MARLENE PARDO PELLICER

The Dead Cast No Shadow

A SIBYL NOVELLA No. 2

The Dead Cast No Shadow

A Sibyl Novella No. 2

Marlene Pardo Pellicer

THE DEAD CAST NO SHADOW: A SIBYL NOVELLA NO. 2. Copyright © Marlene Pardo Pellicer. First Printing 2020. Printed in the United States of America.

First Edition:
First Printing

PUBLISHED BY ELEVENTH HOUR LLC
www.11thhour.company

E-BOOK ISBN 978-1-7348360-3-5
PRINT ISBN 978-1-7348360-4-2

DEDICATION

I dedicate this book to all my fellow countrymen, brave Americans who have faced a very difficult year so far in 2020, but in the spirit of those who hail from the "land of the Free, and the home of the Brave", we will adapt, persevere and overcome.

About The Author

Marlene is a native Miamian and has been writing since 1971, (on a manual typewriter when she was eleven years old).

She is the founder of *Miami Ghost Chronicles*, and a paranormal researcher since the 1990s. She is also the producer, host and narrator of *Stories of the Supernatural*, *Nightshade Diary* and *Supernatural StoryTime* podcast series, and the blog author of *Stranger Than Fiction Stories*.

Marlene lives with her husband Henry (AKA official sandwich maker for starving authors) on a micro-farm and bee sanctuary in Miami's 100-year-old agricultural belt, surrounded by several dogs (AKA writing companions), various noisy exotic birds, and a large flock of equally noisy free-range chickens.

Thelma, the rescue rabbit died July, 2020.

If you'd like to receive my newsletter announcing specials, updates on new books and requests for ideas, please sign up on my website.

www.MarlenePardo.com

Other Books by Marlene

FICTION

I've Come for My Girl and Two Other Dark Tales
(Winter Shade Stories Book 1) (2020)

Sibyl Universe
The Path to Purgatory: Book 2 of the Sibyl Chronicles (2020)
Diabolique: A Sibyl Novella (2019)
Walker Between the Worlds: Book 1 of the Sibyl Chronicles
(2019)

NON-FICTION
Haunted History of the Old West's Wicked Ladies & The Bad
Hombres They Loved (2017)
The Lady in the Blue Kimono: Film Noir Murders (2018)
Supernatural Safety: A Paranormal DIY Guide (2018)

"Now pile your dust upon the quick and the dead . . ."

Hamlet
Shakespeare

Cort:
"There's a click before the strike. Listen to the clock."

The Quick and the Dead
Director: Sam Raimi

References

Sempiterno Apostasy *- A secret sect that infiltrated the Vatican because stories of unearthly and evil creatures were acknowledged and catalogued there. Their members include a select few known as the Dispossessed. Touched by Evil at some time in their lives, their minds were open to the world beyond. They could see its inhabitants, and in turn be seen by them. Who comprised this sect became one of the most sought after secrets in the Vatican. Even the most powerful cardinals and the Inquisition feared them. Members lived in all parts of the world, and their exact number remains unknown even to the Dispossessed themselves.*

Pocket—*a human avatar used by a spiritually advanced being or a demon to disguise their likeness.*

Contents

PROLOGUE

EVERGLADES, FLORIDA 1929.

A thick fog obscured the early morning sun. Frogs and insects replied hopefully to the faint rays of coming daylight. A panther watched with incurious eyes from across a small clearing. She lay under the branches of a large cypress tree satiated from her recent meal of a feral hog. Her indifferent gaze watched a woman with a buttercup yellow dress kneel next to a man sprawled limp on the ground. A slow dribble of blood clotted the soft sand underneath his head. She pulled out a jagged rock he landed on and tossed it aside.

Under her fingers his pulse slowed. In a fluid movement she stood up and stripped off her cardigan sweater, linen chemise, undergarments and finally a straw cloche hat.

She whispered, "I claim you."

Her milk and strawberry nakedness shimmered with a violet cast and she melted into the uniformed figure, evaporating like a thirsty man's mirage. The officer's eyes blinked, and he sat up slowly, fingering the gash at the back of his head. He looked at the bite mark on his hand, and the stream of venom pouring outward from the wound; the cottonmouth it belonged to had long ago slithered into the underbrush.

The only thing left of Officer Kirwin was his body; his spirit gladly flew like an arrow to meet his deceased parents. The man stood up and dusted himself off. He pulled out his handkerchief and blotted the blood from the head wound. He eyed the Harley motorcycle he propped nearby when he stopped to relieve himself.

He took the discarded purse, pulled out a wad of bills and put them in his pocket. He picked up the unwanted clothing and stuffed them behind an island of sawgrass.

Officer Kirwin mounted the motorcycle and rode towards a remote outpost named the Monroe Station. It was one of six stops along the Tamiami Trail that ran east to west between Miami and Naples. It opened only the year before, and while he patrolled the lonely highway, his wife manned a store and gasoline station that offered rest to the road-weary traveler.

Less than an hour before, after he left for patrol, a Boattail Speedster pulled into the station. Mrs. Kirwin made small talk with the driver about the foggy weather as she pumped gasoline into the red convertible. The young man dressed in the latest fashion spoke of continuing his New Year's festivities in Miami. He probably spent the night carousing, she guessed. The faint smell of liquor followed him around like an unseen cloud.

Alcohol was against the law, but living in a place where illegal moonshine stills hid in every remote hammock, she'd learn to keep her mouth shut and look the other way.

Later on, she realized she remembered very little about his companion. She was a red-headed woman with cool green eyes, tanned apricot cheekbones, wearing a pale dress.

The Kirwin family lived on the second floor of the small wooden structure, and she hurried upstairs when her children called out for her, therefore she never saw the woman step out of the vehicle after whispering a few words in the man's ear. He gunned the car and roared off down the road, forgetting entirely that he came this far with a traveling companion he picked up in Naples.

Let the Good Times Roll

ST. PETERSBURG, FLORIDA

"Don't worry, everything's jake." Cole Deyo leaned over and whispered to the waifish blonde woman sitting next to him.

He looked over his shoulder at an attractive brunette with bobbed hair sitting in the back seat of his Dodge Victory. Her serious face showed no expression; even her line thin eyebrows were unexpressive. Now that he got a better look at her, he realized she was older than he estimated. Her rail thin figure and nimbleness on the dance floor had thrown him off. But that didn't matter because she was part of the package.

Georgina the blonde refused to accompany him to Miami unless he agreed to include her friend May. This meant finding a date for her, and that was easier said than done. Too drunk to say no after they staggered out of the last speakeasy was Mickey Pinto, and he was snoring into the cushioned seat of the car next to the miffed brunette.

"Honey, he'll be good as new by the time we roll into Miami, I promise." He winked at May. "All you have to do is relax and enjoy the ride."

Without a smile, she shrugged her shoulder and replied, "I don't care, as long as he doesn't barf on my shoes."

Cole threw his head back, guffawed and then nuzzled Georgina's rouged cheek, "Did you hear honey? Now she's on the trolley!"

3

He'd run a shipment of rum from Miami to Naples, and up to St. Petersburg two days before, but now he needed to head back to the east coast. Just when he was getting ready to leave he'd met this little tomato, and when she told him she was a nurse over at Faith Hospital, erotic scenes of her dressed in white burrowed into his brain and then shot down to his cock.

Cole finally convinced her to accompany him, but she insisted May, another nurse, come along.

He slid back over to his side of the seat, pulled the clutch and the car rocketed off down the road. Dawn promised to break over the horizon soon, and he envisioned spending the rest of the day between the sheets with sweet Georgina.

* * *

The Dodge Victory idled outside an imposing iron wrought gate surrounded by pink crescents of bougainvillea flowers. A red-tiled house, a replica from one on the Mediterranean coast, rose beyond it.

Cole Deyo waited and smoked a cigarette. A short, balding man exited from an arched doorway. His clothing was crisp and uncreased, and he smelled faintly of aftershave from his freshly scraped face. His voice was low and steady, and Cole wondered if the man celebrated New Year's Eve at all.

"Bring the same amount in two weeks, and I'll need double as much for February. Can you supply it?"

"Yeah, sure, I told you I'm good for it."

"Very well, in two weeks then."

The man nodded, stepped away towards the entrance, then stopped and turned back. "Be careful of those new stops on the Tamiami Trail. They have police pulling speeding cars over; they need to make up the money it cost for the road construction. Most of those cops are new and want to make sure they keep their jobs."

Cole lit another cigarette and muttered, "Thanks."

Two years ago a hurricane slammed into Miami, and the economy suffered for it. The booming real estate business tanked and crippled many of the local businesses in South Florida. Those who secured a job, did whatever it took to keep it, because there were plenty ready to step in and take their place.

The thin man with the mussed linen suit took a long pull from the cigarette, and squashed a premonition of unease that filled him. This stop in Naples was a secret he kept from his boss in Miami; a little side action for extra income.

He dropped off two cases and didn't expect the guy would want more, but these rich types didn't want to slum it in a speakeasy. It seemed there was more money on the table than he originally thought.

He tossed the cigarette away and decided he needed some sleep. As if on cue, Mickey sat up and stared at him with watery, bloodshot eyes. He motioned him to the front seat. The women exchanged places and the last thing he remembered was placing his head on Georgina's lap and thinking to himself, "All I have to be is a little smarter, and a lot faster."

* * *

May Jackson watched the hazy swamp fall away on either side of the narrow road as the automobile sped down the road. Mist crept low across the land and an occasional egret stared after their progress as it stood in the shallow waters hunting its next meal.

Her body leaned into the car door, ignoring the pasty-faced man who threw occasional but speculative glances in her direction. Her body language made it clear she was not interested in conversation, much less romance.

There was only one reason she agreed to a three-hour trip with Georgina and two bootleggers. She needed to reconnoiter if Miami would be her next home.

She'd learned by now that movement was essential, and not when thing turned bad, but when everything was good. And things were good, but many years passed since she sensed that sickening premonition warning her away from her post. She always heeded it without a second thought.

As a nurse, she'd never encountered a problem finding a job. Her employers thought of her as reliable and most importantly of good moral character. When asked about her unmarried state, she would make a vague reference to the death of her one true love in the Great War, and that would end all inquiries.

Her plans were to stay the winter in St. Petersburg, which would be full of those fleeing the icy winds of the northern states, but something changed in the last week. Certitude filled her being that if she waited it would be too late, and she'd learned by now not to measure it with logic, but simply to act and place distance between herself and the last place she called home.

Viewing the green darkness of the endless miles of watery marshes, she analyzed what she felt. This exercise was rare for her, because she rarely dissected her feelings, but it served her well since she was unflinching in her examination. Something hunted her; by whom or what, she didn't know, but curiosity did not raise its insistent head, only that she must lose her status as a quarry immediately.

Then she thought of Mrs. Pettigrew. She'd been so patient and careful with this one; part of her rebelled in abandoning the woman when she was so close to claiming her. She'd figured out just the right amount of morphine to administer so she would stop breathing. This was a change of methods and it was futile to deny the thrill that ran through her body. The last two she asphyxiated with a pillow, and the anticipation she'd enjoyed was like the most potent aphrodisiac.

But what was that saying about living to fight another day? But, in her case, it was kill another day.

She always made sure to be present when the family or friends would arrive at the hospital to be told of the death. Their grief and disbelief held her spellbound. The best were the ones when she would stand patiently next to the doctor when he broke the news. Sometimes she pretended to comfort the grieving, watching those around her dancing to the rhythm of anguish she set in motion.

She ignored those bereft of friends and families. Only when the needs for funds demanded it, as in when she was planning to move, she would choose one that in their loneliness would be garrulous about money they kept stashed somewhere. With patience, she would extract information from them and steal it at an appropriate time. She never took jewelry or anything that could be traced to the deceased person. So far, this formula worked like a charm.

The Allison Hospital in Miami Beach, built to cater to the wealthy families who wintered there, was taken over by the Sisters of St. Francis. Renamed the St. Francis Hospital she considered seeking employment there.

Her eyes flicked towards Mickey, who offered her a cigarette and a half-hearted grimace. Internally, she debated how unpleasant she could be with him now. What if she used him for transportation using the pretext of sightseeing in a new city?

So she smiled at him, a soft flirty lifting of her thin lips. He continued to stare at her, realizing she was much prettier than the fake blonde sitting with Cole in the back. When his eyes returned to the road, they widened and his face paled in alarm.

The sickening motion of the automobile followed as it lost its center of gravity and rolled. It caused her to grab the door handle and her other hand braced against the roof. She saw a figure mounted on a motorcycle bounce from the left front wheel of the car and a man's figure fly through the air as they continued in their roll. The screech of rubber and crunch of metal followed their path through space as they rotated completely. Miraculously, the car righted itself.

Mickey and May looked at each other. Blood spread down his face from a deep cut on the bridge of his nose, and she looked down at her bruised knuckles. She released her death grip on the dashboard and her hand trembled violently.

They both turned around when Cole shouted in their ear, "Where is she? Where the fuck is she?" The back seat was empty except for him.

Passengers

The rolling vehicle discharged Georgina's thin body out the open window in a graceful ballet, choreographed in the split second of impact with the policeman's motorcycle. Her body followed an inevitable trajectory that would have broken her back against the thick trunk of a nearby sycamore tree, except that arms caught and swung her around. But it was only her flesh and blood saved as her soul honored the pact made when she grew in her mother's womb that this would be the moment of her death.

Nearby Officer Kirwin's body lay lifeless, and later an autopsy would find he died from a fractured skull. None would think to test him for the vestiges of venom that were the true reason for his demise.

For the second time that day, the Walker Between the Worlds existed inside a body that was not her own, but this time it was different. Granted only seven days to use it, then it would generate all the injuries it sustained if she had not intervened. The wounds would not only have killed Georgina, but left her body unusable and broken; unable to walk or breathe.

Yells came from the car, and she lay down and rolled in the dirt, scratching herself.

"I'm here," she called out in a feeble voice.

They ran to her, and she sat up slowly.

A few minutes later a car rolled up on the scene. The motorist agreed to drive to the next station and call for help. They took the four of them to the hospital in the small town of Everglades. They were released after being treated for cuts and bruises. Their incredible good fortune even extended to the Dodge Victory, which could be driven after a few blows to the side fender.

9

Wounded and gassed during the World War, they took officer Kirwin to a funeral home in Miami. The inquest held by Sheriff Thorpe found that the fog caused him to strike the vehicle. Later the sheriff gave Mrs. Kirwin all the money found in the policeman's pockets. He refused to speculate how the man, after only working eight months in this post, gathered this amount of cash. He was just happy he could give the widow and her two children money to subsist on.

* * *

The drive into Miami was quiet. The sun was setting when the Dodge arrived at the Halcyon Hotel located on NE Second Avenue and Flagler Street. Cole spoke to the concierge and secured a room for the two women. He handed them some money, wished them luck and left them to decide whether to use the money to stay longer in Miami or buy fare to travel back to St. Petersburg.

In a transformation he could not explain the desire that engulfed him when he met Georgina evaporated and he now considered her a jinx. There was something about her that set his teeth on edge.

Aware they survived a serious accident, the concierge thoughtfully took them to a small dress shop on the first floor occupied by retail businesses so they were able to purchase clean clothing.

This action was not all together altruistic, since Cole left money for this purpose. That there was no bar or alcohol served in the hotel. This allowed him to make a tidy profit from buying liquor for guests who wanted to quietly imbibe in their rooms. The bootlegger was a reliable supplier, so it was in his best interest to stay on his good side.

He allowed them time to make their choices and even escorted them to their room, refusing a tip. The door closed behind both women as they wandered around, marveling at the richly furnished room.

"Are you ready to go back to work?" Georgina asked, smiling at May, her thin face twisted into white teeth and wide brown eyes.

May shook her head and sat back in a comfortable chair, fingering the cushioned armrests. "I'm not sure what I'm ready for." Her stomach churned, a sure sign her nerves were still on edge.

A knock on the door interrupted the conversation and when they opened it, a hotel employee wheeled in a tray with food which comprised Chicken à la King over rice, and pineapple upside-down cake.

"With compliments of the hotel ladies," the fresh-scrubbed young man said, and refused a tip. He left and closed the door smartly behind him.

Georgina slid a chair over to the rolling tray and dug out a napkin and plate. "So, what's bothering you, aren't you hungry?"

"What?" May asked, distaste running across her features as she looked at the food.

Georgina eyed her in silence for a moment. "May, we have eaten nothing for a day." Then she took a serving spoon and filled her plate, licking her fingers off after inhaling deeply of the still steaming food.

May shook her head. The Georgina she knew would have been climbing the walls for a cigarette, and wondering if her lipstick was bright and red, not salivating over a hefty plate of food.

May stood up reluctantly and joined Georgina at the table. The smell was heavenly, but she jerked, almost dropping the serving spoon when she looked up suddenly and saw intense green eyes looking through her. She blinked, and by then Georgina was looking down into her plate, and when she looked up once more, the eyes were the same plain brown.

11

"I'm wondering," May said, then stopped and looked down at the empty plate.

"Wondering what?" Georgina asked, chewing a mouthful of food.

May looked her directly in the eye. "I'm wondering if you're okay."

"Sure, beyond a couple of scratches." She took another mouthful and wiped her hands. Georgina wasn't really pushing, but she harbored a hunch she would find out quickly what was bothering May and what she planned to do now.

"I don't think I'm going back to St. Petersburg," May said. "I'd been considering it before, but I guess I'm more shook up than I care to admit. Maybe this accident was a sign I should stay here now."

Georgina raised her eyebrows in surprise. "Not returning to St. Petersburg?"

"Would you mind packing up my clothing and sending it over to me once you get back?"

"Go chase yourself! I'd been thinking of doing the same thing."

Georgina's words were like a punch in the gut. May pushed back slightly from the table. What little appetite surfaced disappeared. A lump in her throat, made it difficult to swallow.

The last thing she wanted was a tie between her and St. Petersburg. This was a serious impediment she had not expected.

Georgina leaned forward, staring at May with a puzzled look. "What's wrong?" She must have been able to read the other woman's reaction and her discomfort with the direction of the conversation.

"You've never mentioned this before." May said.

"Like you, I'd just been twirling it round in my head." She ate another mouthful and nodded. "I'm sure we can land a job quick over here."

12

THE DEAD CAST NO SHADOW

May sat back. "Are you sure you want to live here?" she asked, looking at the unworried expression on the other woman's face. "What about those beaus romancing you; I thought you were serious about them? Seemed they wanted to put a ring on your finger. You will leave behind the chance for the white picket fence deal?"

Georgina nodded. "That's the whole point; they haven't gone down on one knee and asked 'the question'. And the truth is, there's no sizzle. I think Mr. Right is here in Miami. We can ask Minnie to send our things over, and we'll plead poverty to Nurse Deets and tell her we have no money to go back."

May had little if any sense of humor, but she admitted to herself she like being around Georgina because she was blunt, funny and pragmatic when bad things happened to people. She wasn't sentimental like most of the other nurses working at Faith Hospital. However, one thing Georgina lacked was true intelligence, but now it seemed she developed not only smarts but a sense of purpose.

Georgina kept eating with gusto, then stopped and cocked her head to one side. "I'm surprised you'd want to leave Faith Hospital. I took you for one of those married-to-their-job types. When you first arrived, I thought you were a bluenose."

May cleared her throat and cut a sliver of the pineapple-upside down cake. "But a girl's gotta look out for herself. There's more opportunity here."

"That's what I thought too. No offense May, but you're a soft touch with some patients. Especially those wailin' like banshees about pain. For instance, Mrs. Pettigrew, you're always there by her bedside when she starts with her sniffling and complaints."

That froze May with the fork halfway to her mouth. She looked intensely at the other woman.

Finally she asked, "Are you joking?"

13

"No joke," Georgina said, staring into her glittering, fierce eyes. "The other nurses think you're a wurp, but your secret's safe with me."

May put the fork down and wiped off her hands, then her mouth, shaking her head the entire time as thoughts raced through her mind.

"I just hate the noise, that's all."

"Well, okay." Georgina smiled at her, reached over and cut a slice of the dessert. "Both ways, here we are now, and the New Year's turning out to be quite an adventure." She shrugged her thin shoulders and smiled at the dark haired woman who stared down at her lap.

May looked up and said, "I'll go back to St. Petersburg and get our things."

Georgina smiled thoughtfully and replied, "Sure, sounds like a good idea. We'll ask tomorrow morning about the cheapest fare back over there, and in the meantime I'll visit the hospital and ask if they're hiring nurses."

May nodded, thinking about where she would leave to once she returned to Faith Hospital.

The conversation ended as Georgina kept eating and May left with the pretext of buying cigarettes from a shop downstairs.

The blonde woman smiled at her. "Great, that's what I need 'bout now." Then she winked at May.

Both women sought their beds early that night considering the events of the day. After midnight Georgina heard May move around. She pretended to be sleeping and through her lashes saw May standing at the foot of the bed, just staring at her intensely.

May decided something that both excited and scared her to death. She would not return to St. Petersburg after all; instead she would kill Georgina. All she needed to figure out was how, but it

THE DEAD CAST NO SHADOW

had to be soon. Perhaps being in a city where they were strangers would prove to be a significant advantage.

Late Night Moon

Georgina nibbled on a toast covered in butter, and with a red-tipped fingernail, pointed at a small ad in the newspaper.

Rooms for Rent
> *Flagler and 17th Court. $2 a week. Hot water in each room. Also 2-room apt. $15 month 35 N.W. 17th Court. Phone 33383.*

"Look May, that's near to here, and we have enough money to pay for a week." She tossed the newspaper to the dark-haired woman that stared vacantly out the window.

May took the paper, opened it and eyed the front-page stories. She'd overslept, and her body ached all over. For many years in the privacy of her room, she'd made a habit of reading all the stories about crimes, especially murders. She'd learned a great deal about police procedure and who got caught and why.

Georgina hummed annoyingly and slurped her coffee. Then in a perky voice she rattled off, "I went downstairs early this morning and they let me use the phone when I explained about the accident. I called the hospital and told Nurse Deets what happened; for once she softened up and told me we could take the rest of the week off. I thought I'd leave out the part that we were partying with a couple of rum runners, and that we have plans of staying here."

The newspaper rattled in May's hands. In the past Georgina would have pleaded with the older woman to be the one to make the phone call and get them off the hook with the head nurse who ruled the staff with an iron first.

In fact, Georgina did what she would have done. By getting word to the hospital, it avoided a hornet's nest being stirred up if they notified the police about two missing nurses. Instead, she would have related to the powers that be the story she wanted to feed them. Carefully picked words guaranteed a huge dollop of pity to be their reward. She still felt annoyed that Georgina became independent of her, and once more the thoughts that kept her awake all during the night came back to her with a fresh edge to them.

The curtain at an open window fluttered in a cool breeze coming in from the ocean. With it drifted the shouts of men, accompanied by the sound of hammers and saws. Now that the New Year's holiday was over, construction crews returned to their work.

May stood at the window and looked at them milling about. They were building an enormous edifice, and her eyes drifted down to huge pits being dug and quarry stones being lined up for the walls of the structure. She envisioned hitting Georgina over the head with a blunt object and shoving her into one of the holes.

"Could the solution be that easy?" she asked herself. She pushed the idea aside, but didn't dismiss it outright.

From across the room Georgina pretended to smoke a cigarette, leaving it to burn in a nearby ashtray. The being named Ema that existed within the blonde woman's thin frame observed May with unrelenting eyes.

Little did May suspect that Ema understood more about her than any other living human being.

* * *

SAVANNAH, GEORGIA 1920.

An old man, with faltering steps and the aid of a cane, left his buggy and doddered painfully to the crossroads of four remote country roads. He carried a burlap bag with him. A full moon riding high among a few shredded clouds illuminated the area, and with the tip of the cane he drew a circle around him. From inside the bag he drew out a black chicken with its legs tied. He threw it on the ground and pulled out other packets specially prepared for him. The supplicant muttered words of incantation, but he possessed the most potent of aids, which was the absolute belief in the existence of the being he came to conjure this night.

He waited; the stillness of the night broken only by the sounds of insects and animals that carried on during this time of darkness. He strained his hearing, hoping to catch the sibilant whisper of his name, "Levan Jackson," to announce the one he sought.

His mouth became dry in a mixture of despair and anticipation. It brought to mind the year he came to Washington D.C. to apprentice with an undertaker acquainted with his family. The man agreed to train him after the unexpected death of his father. He was eleven years old and before the month was out, Mr. Montgomery, his employer repeatedly raped him. Levan knew why the man treated him thus. His mother, burdened with eight other children, made it clear the man could do whatever he wanted with him. Everything except return him to her.

However, Levan soon learned where Mr. Montgomery's true passion lay. It was with the dead bodies that came to his establishment. A few months after his arrival, the Civil War started, and the amount of dead increased. Once the bodies were delivered at H. Montgomery Undertaker, family members would have been appalled to discover the indignities suffered by their loved ones.

It wasn't only dead soldiers that came to them, but the victims of typhoid, dysentery and malaria that flourished from the trash strewn street of Washington D.C.

Mr. Montgomery brought him to his bed occasionally, but there came a time where the man became more titillated from having Levan witness his actions with the dead instead. It was during one of these episodes he saw a shadowy figure that hovered close by

18

THE DEAD CAST NO SHADOW

Mr. Montgomery. Man-like it had the head of a dog, with two horns, droopy goat ears and the hindquarters of a bovine along with hooves.

It visited him in his dreams; communicating with strange and disturbing images. It told him to be patient that soon it would take him as an apprentice because Montgomery was an inferior being. It waited for many years for one like him; and it would reward him with everything he desired.

One night Levan accompanied Mr. Montgomery to meet with a university anatomist willing to pay for corpses so their students could dissect them. The doctor told him he would leave it up to his discretion which ones to pick, hopefully those with little or no family to interfere, and that the body should be as intact as possible.

Undertakers performed the tasks of removing, transporting and preparing the dead for burial, and with Montgomery's lack of conscience it became a thriving business.

The war ended, and Levan realized that he craved the respectability afforded to the physicians of the day. He was sixteen years old and took an older doctor as a lover. Married with several children, none were aware of his double life. Levan convinced him via a hint of blackmail to find him a spot in the university as a student.

The young undertaker was literate, intelligent and ambitious. When he told Mr. Montgomery of his plans, the man protested. Then his apprentice jumped across the dinner table and held a knife to his throat, promising to gut him in slow measure and to keep him alive during the procedure. Fear engulfed Montgomery. Weakness came over him like a tidal wave. He saw the strength and cunning he once enjoyed, shining from Levan's eyes.

H. Montgomery Undertaker continued to operate those years that Levan studied. The owner suffered in poverty, turning over all his earnings to his onetime apprentice who lived a lavish lifestyle.

Upon graduation, Dr. Levan Jackson realized that Mr. Montgomery, and the business were a liability. One day the char woman found the undertaker hanging from a rope and the business promptly closed afterwards. They listed suicide as the cause of death. Levan strangled the man during several hours while he ate a hearty meal and drank assorted bottles of vintage wine.

The years rolled by and Dr. Jackson established a thriving practice and became well-respected among his peers. He taught classes at the university and he occasionally took a student as a lover. But like Montgomery, he found true fulfillment from dead bodies. Their appeal would start when the person was alive, and sometimes he found ways of hastening death to consummate his obsession. None would think to question orders from a physician to be left alone with his patient, dead or alive.

It was the morning of his fiftieth birthday, and the year was 1900 when he overheard a conversation between his housekeeper and the cook. The gist of the gossip was that contrary to his belief that many considered him a wealthy, but eccentric bachelor, in truth his reputation was being ruined because of his preference for the company of handsome, young men.

He realized there was only one remedy, which was marriage. He searched for a particular bride; one on the brink of spinsterhood but young enough to bear children, from a respectable background but impoverished with little or no family who would interfere in their relationship. There was one quality that he prized above all others, which was meekness and unflinching loyalty to the marriage bonds. He found everything he sought with Marie Van Beek, who was a companion to her grandaunt Geraldine Van Beek of New York. The match enticed him with the added incentive that Marie would inherit Mrs. Van Beek's small fortune.

Once Marie became pregnant during the first year of their marriage, he never came to her bed again. The damaging whispers about him disappeared, and before their first anniversary Mrs. Jackson gave birth to a daughter, they named May.

The next crisis came when Marie unexpectedly committed suicide five years later with an overdose of laudanum. Dr. Jackson who understood only too well the stigma of suicide within a family concocted a story about his wife's weak heart, and they listed this as the cause of death.

He hired a governess to look after his daughter and teach her the proper etiquette of the day. Engrossed in his work and his passions which were the dead and an occasional lover from among his peers, or a student seeking to ingratiate himself for a better grade, he again overlooked the signs that Miss Smith the governess noticed something about him was off. Firing her would have been easy, but he didn't need a disgruntled, suspicious ex-employee to seek revenge by spreading rumors.

He never cut ties with the murky underworld of criminals and murderers, and it was easy to find someone to kill Miss Smith and chop up her body for the right amount of money.

He studied several notebooks the woman wrote her lessons in and copied her handwriting. They found a short note stating she ran away with an unnamed soldier and they were seeking their fortune somewhere in California. Again, his status as a doctor and a pillar of the community guaranteed no one would question what happened to the little governess.

May was ten years old when he started to molest her; repeating the cycle of what Montgomery did to him by having her witness his desecration of corpses. To his surprise though, he found his daughter was very intelligent, and so he also shared with her his medical knowledge.

Then came the first time in his life that he fell dangerously in love; it was with a young soldier almost fifty years his junior. His lover bilked him out of most of his fortune, and for once he did not care about his reputation. He lost his practice and faced the disgrace of moving out of Washington, D.C. His young lover died in Europe; the victim of friendly fire one month shy of the end of war in 1918.

One day he came home to find May waiting for him with her bags packed. She forced him to compose a letter of recommendation on the university letterhead confirming she was a competent nurse. He looked into her eyes and realized she took something he prized more than any of the riches he had lost. It was the spirit of the creature which accompanied him since those early years as Montgomery's apprentice.

He came out of a trance, where he revisited all those events of his life. He opened his eyes and inhaled sharply when a tall woman draped in a blood red cloak stood outside the circle looking at him. This was not what he expected, but perhaps this was a masquerade the creature used.

His first doubt came when she asked, "Where is May now?"

"I don't know," he mumbled, "she's never communicated with me."

She strode forward, and with her foot obliterated the circle he created only minutes before. She shoved him hard into the ground and stood over him. "I came looking for the same thing you have, and I will punish you with a prophecy so your trip will not be wasted. You will live another eight years and suffer from several painful illnesses that affect your digestive system and your bones. There will come a time that morphine will not give you relief, but death will not come for you. When you die, it will be in poverty, covered in your filth, in extreme pain, alone and forgotten."

The woman bent down and freed the chicken. With purposeful steps she stalked to his scrawny horse, untied the leads to the buggy and mounted it. With soft words she urged it forward, and disappeared into the murkiness of the road.

* * *

So with knowing eyes, Ema looked at May's back, guessing her plans. This did not worry her. What did, was the fact that in six days Georgina's body would die from all the injuries she temporarily staved off. This, and when the demon existing inside its human avatar realized the blonde woman was the pocket of the Walker Between the Worlds.

Unlikely Allies

May got into the taxi cab and told the driver to take her to the Frolics Cabaret. This was the place Mickey Pinto told her he would be if she changed her mind about seeing him before she left Miami.

Georgina stayed behind with plans to visit the room advertised for rent.

When she arrived, the place stood shuttered and quiet. She knocked and a skinny, boyish woman answered the door. She wore an apron and smelled of disinfectant. The woman looked her up and down when she asked for Mickey, and said, "All right hon', just wait right here."

A few minutes later, Mickey opened the door and stood there for a moment, surprised to see her. A wiry man, with a premature receding hairline, his nervous eyes constantly scanned around him. His nose was purple and swollen from the injury caused in the accident.

May reminded herself to stay calm and controlled, analyzing what she needed to do to manipulate Mickey to do what she wanted. Now was not the time to be aloof.

"Well, didn't think I'd see you again," Mickey was saying, "but I ain't gonna complain."

May used a keen power of observation that she honed for several years, interpreting clues invisible to normal people. She understood and expected behavior that many would consider uncanny if she admitted to what she knew within seconds of meeting someone.

"I was hoping you liked surprises."

"Surprises," Mickey nodded, looking at her with a lascivious gleam in his eye, "that look like you is my absolute favorite."

24

May thanked him for the compliment with a hint of bashfulness.

"Wanna go back to my apartment and have a drink?" he suggested to her. "Perhaps lunch afterward?"

"Sure." May responded.

He turned back inside and shouted instructions to someone. A few minutes later a teenage boy drove a shiny car to the front. He came around and opened the door for May while Mickey settled himself behind the wheel.

When they came to the end of the block, he stopped and pulled her next to him. "You don't talk a whole lot, do you?" Mickey asked. "It's all right, we'll pretend we just met and we need to get to know one another."

May nodded and settled her frame under his arm, forcing herself to relax the muscles of her shoulders. She abhorred dry conversations, and the allure of small talk escaped her. But she reminded herself that silence; even companionable silence did not seduce men.

She'd overheard what they said behind her back. That she was too quiet and unfriendly.

"I've never been here before," she said at last, in a low voice.

"Yeah, I keep forgetting that."

Mickey's apartment turned out to be a cozy cottage, and he pulled the car into a side garage. May slipped away because she guessed his intention was to kiss her. She did this because she saw that he enjoyed a good chase, and if she submitted he would probably have thrown up her skirt in the car, had sex with her and then driven back to the Frolics Cabaret.

Once inside, he made them a drink and settled in for the pursuit. May flirted with an effort, which intrigued him even more. She listened with feigned interest to his stories about running the supper club, and she even convinced him to allow her to make them sandwiches for lunch. She understood he expected they would end up in the bedroom, but in the meantime he enjoyed having a woman listen to him, making him the center of attention.

During a pause in the conversation, she became serious and stopped smiling.

"Hey what's wrong?" he asked.

"Well Mickey, you know, I'd been thinking of coming to Miami even before the accident and getting a job at a hospital."

He nodded, wondering where the conversation was going.

"But, I thought I owed you and Cole a favor considering you made sure we had a place to stay."

He listened in silence.

She continued, "Fact is, that Georgina's been acting weird. Her family is one of those teetotalers, and I think she hit her head in the accident, 'cause she keeps talking about how she owes God since he spared her life. She's sorry about her sinful ways and drinkin' and all."

"I could think of worse New Year's resolutions," he murmured, "but what's that got to do with anything?"

"Well, she's got some uncle that's a G-Man and she was telling me that God wants her to be right with the laws of man too. She's got this cockamamie idea she's gonna tell him everything she'd seen. She mentioned you both."

At this, Mickey sat up in his seat.

"She even remembered the address we stopped at in Naples."

"She does, does she?"

May stood up and unbuttoned her dress. She took him by the hand and led him into the bedroom, making him forget about her story.

As she expected, he pushed up her slip, unzipped his pants and engaged in quick intercourse with her. Despite his claim that he ran the cabaret she suspected he could not disappear for the entire afternoon.

THE DEAD CAST NO SHADOW

Once he finished she murmured to him, "You know honey, I just wanted to make sure you knew that I have nothing to do with any trouble she can stir up for you fellas."

"So when is she leaving?"

"I think tomorrow, we don't have any money left, so she did me a favor and went to check on a rental room being advertised before she took the bus back."

He stood up and straightened up his clothing. He reached into his pocket and threw several bills on the bed. "That should cover you for the rest of the week at the hotel. Convince her to stay for a few more days. Then I suggest you get your job at the hospital. and pretend you never even heard her name."

May gazed at him and smiled in understanding. "Sure honey, mum's the word."

Mickey dropped her off in front of the hotel and then sped off. After counting the money she realized he gave her more than she needed for the hotel. She knew it was hush money. At the front desk she extended their stay for two more days. She hoped that Georgina would disappear by then and she would have even more money to start her life in Miami.

When she returned to the room, she found Georgina sipping an ice tea, accompanied by a soup and salad.

Georgina volunteered, "Hey the room was already rented, but the landlady said she might have one available next week and told me to check back."

"I found some extra money in my purse and I think we've got enough to stay at the hotel for a few more days. Why don't you hold off on leaving yet and keep me company? Nurse Deets doesn't expect you back until next week right?"

"Sure, I could get used to this real easy." Georgina replied brightly and continued eating.

May turned away smiling. This was the Georgina she knew; wholly ignorant of how much it cost to stay in a hotel of this caliber. There was no way either of them could scrape enough money to cover even one more day.

She excused herself to step into the bathroom.

Georgina continued to eat her food, but now with a thoughtful look on her face. May failed to realize she followed her in another taxicab and saw when it dropped her off in front of the Frolics Cabaret. The reason for the visit posed no mystery. Now she had a bull's eye on her, but did she expect any less from a woman that held no remorse in her heart?

Unpredictable and Dangerous

May was lying in bed awake. The tightness in her chest and trouble drawing in a breath woke her. She tried to swallow the lump in her throat. She fought the sensation like a drowning person seeking the surface, and she gasped when she finally filled her lungs. With the first gulp of oxygen came the stink; an odor that translated into a taste inside her mouth. She wasn't sure which was worse, the stench or the inability to breath.

Her labored inhalation filled the silence in the room, and when a faint scratching sounded out from under her bed, the noise was distinct. May rarely remembered her dreams, and the dread that filled her being made her wonder if she was not awake. The scratching, slow and deliberate continued.

There was a pop as if pieces of flesh were detaching one from the other with a slow, slurping effort; tissue, ligaments and muscle fighting separation. Something else in the room panted, spluttered and clicked.

There was a thought that filled her mind with unmistakable certainty, "She smells me."

Hard on the heels of this thought, the noise became more frenetic. "She's excited."

May's eyes swiveled over to the side of the bed where she met shiny orbs that stared into hers. A long tongue danced and dabbed at a cracked lower lip, while the wet-looking eyes rolled upwards into its head. Startled May realized it looked like her, but not quite human, but even in the dark the similarity was undeniable.

The creature swayed back and forth, and her bulging eyeballs which were only black pupils surrounded by bloodshot veins came to meet her stare once again. Then came the moment where she turned up the corners of her mouth in a failed attempt at a smile.

The creature pulled herself out from under the frame and edged forward on all fours, until she came to the foot of the bed, and placed her forearms and bony shoulders on the covering. Her hair was dirty, tangled and hung in patches from a gray scalp. Skeletal fingers that ended in long, yellow nails pulled her forward. For a moment, May thought she had four-fingered hands until she saw that both of her thumbs were cut off where they joined the hand, and only bloody stumps were left. The wounds dribbled blood.

The contorted body crawled forward towards May. Occasionally she would lick the place where her thumbs once were, and then she would roll her eyes backwards again in ecstasy. Inch by inch she moved over May's legs, and as she got closer to her face her excitement increased and she started once again to pant. Only rags covered her body, and the surface of her skin flaked with dirt and dry blood.

May's voice caught in her throat and try as she might to move her limbs they would not obey her command. Fear, she believed had been burned out of her during childhood, now deluged her being to the core.

The May Creature glared at her through strands of stringy hair, and then it made retching noises. One of her four-fingered hands disappeared into her mouth, as she continued to gag. It withdrew a pendant with a chain covered in thick saliva. It belonged to Annabelle Smith her governess, who gave it to her many years ago before she disappeared.

The creature spoke in a deep, scratchy voice, "Once I got her out of the way, I claimed you. I strengthened and emboldened you. Without me, your father became weak. I left him for you, and you saw what happened to him. I have protected you all these years, and now you are blind."

Each consonant and syllable that poured from its mouth caused a strident pain in each of May's ears.

"She hunts us, she hunts me!" The creature shrieked.

May whimpered in agony, and a warm trickle of blood dribbled out from each ear.

"Who?" May croaked.

"The Sibyl!"

The dark-haired woman stared at the creature in both pain and incomprehension.

"She is close."

Georgina's groggy voice sounded out from the other bed in the room, "May, who are you talking to?"

"Help me."

"Sure sugar. Whew, it smells bad in here!"

Overpowering pressure and weight pinned May's lower body down. The creature hissed in discontent, and she wondered if the light would awaken her from the worse nightmare of her life.

The bedclothes rustled as Georgina sat up in bed, and then she clicked on the lamp sitting on the nightstand. She was facing away, and May's eyes darted between the hissing thing draped across her body, and the tousled head of the woman who seemed deaf.

Finally Georgina stood up and turned around. She crossed her arms, and said in her perky and irritating voice, "Well, there's something you don't see every day."

In an instant May was free. The inability to move disappeared, and she fell off the bed. A rage-filled growl sounded down from the corner of the ceiling, and she followed Georgina's stare to see the demon crouched in the darkest corner. Its eyes glimmered with hatred.

On legs that wobbled, May crawled over the bed towards Georgina. She sensed an emptiness in her body as if her innards were sloshing around inside.

31

Once she stood next to the thin, blonde woman, she felt safe.

The thing in the darkness writhed in impotence and rage. It cried out in a throaty moan, "May, come here."

The dark-haired woman threw herself down on the bed, covering her ears with her hands, the pain driving her towards the edge of sanity.

"We'll have no more of that." May heard a voice come from Georgina that was not hers. In an instant the agony bouncing around inside her skull ceased. She cowed amongst the rumpled bedclothes Georgina abandoned only moments before.

"She is mine, return her." The May Creature demanded.

"No." was the simple reply.

The thing screeched low and deep.

"You will leave now, and this woman is under my protection."

May covered her head, and when she looked up again, her gut tightened up in shock. Georgina's body lay stretched out on the floor; limp and lifeless. Where she stood only moments before was a tall, red-haired woman. She had never seen her before, except in a second she recognized the green eyes as the ones that stared at her from Georgina's face a day before.

Ema knew the demon was as much a slave to its avatar as it claimed to be the master. The only thing that kept it here now was this hunger to claim the being it used for so many years.

"She will never be yours," Ema said in an unflinching tone.

The words created the effect she intended, in a second the creature launched itself downwards towards May, who screamed in terror. Like a child she covered her head again and never saw the sword that winked like a star in Ema's hand. It sliced downward in a flash, severing the demon's head.

The headless body bounced around on the ground, like a child having a tantrum the arms and legs thumped in frenetic disarray.

THE DEAD CAST NO SHADOW

In a corner, the head closed and opened its mouth like a fish out of water. The stench of rotted blood filled every part of the room.

Once the fiend manifested itself in the physical world, it was subject to the laws of this dimension, and the power of Ema's sword, Zeruko Neskamea, forged and inscribed with prayers could cleave it as easily as a human body.

In those moments, when May became liberated from the creature that drove her towards murder and deceit, the years of despair and guilt flooded over her.

Now her soul became filled with another agony that she could not bear as she recalled everything done to her, and that she in turn committed upon others.

She stood up, and Ema whispered, "May, don't."

The woman responded, "I must." Without another word she ran towards the open window and launched herself outward from the fifth floor of the hotel. The sound of her body hitting the pavement followed a few seconds later.

At that instant a rapid knock sounded at the door. "Please open up at once," a muffled voice said sharply.

Ema sighed. She'd hoped May's choice would have been different, but she could not interfere with her actions.

With a quick flick of her wrist, she opened a slit in the fabric of this time and place with her Toledo sword. Out filed two cowled figures. They bowed their heads to her, and each stooped to take a portion of the demonic being.

An angel came through the opening. He appeared as an older man with silver, shoulder-length hair and a full beard. Armor protected his chest, and a powerful sword hung on his belt.

He stopped the figure holding the May creature's head and pulled out a pulsing pearl.

He turned to Ema, "Sibyllina, you have been hunting this one for a long time. You are relentless as always, but your sorrow weighs you down. Your wrath which is the bane of hell will not soothe your heart. Do not let it blind you."

"I will consider your words." Ema said with finality. The hotel manager would return soon with a key to open the door, especially with the discovery of May's body.

Each figure stepped back in through the slit which glowed with a bright, incandescent light beyond it. The angel looked at her meaningfully before he stepped through and the tear mended itself.

Inside the closet, Ema pulled out a new outfit May purchased earlier, which still lay wrapped inside tissue paper. The sizing was appropriate for her, and she clothed her naked body moments before the room door swung open.

She cast a momentary glamour over herself which made her invisible to the manager and another employee. She slipped out the door behind them and walked down the hallway. Their exclamations of alarm followed her as she made her way to the elevator. Outside, a ring of people gathered around May's body, and someone draped a coat over the corpse. She meandered away in the opposite direction.

A lesson she learned ages ago was the inability of a demon to communicate with its avatar would draw it forth. Without its pocket it was powerless in this world. Interfering in this communication and the spiritual bondage it held the human in would create an infallible provocation. She began her efforts as soon as May returned from her conversation with Mickey Pinto.

She sighed, for she recalled the words of the angel, and the grief in her heart was as strident and sharp as ever. This year marked a decade since Mort Peccatum, her last sentient avatar died of old age. They'd hunted together for close to seventy years.

She reminded herself she was human, and like so many of her kind she opted to sooth her sadness with the balm of anger, only to find out the relief was temporary.

THE DEAD CAST NO SHADOW

The winter sun peeked over the horizon when she came to a diner with an outdoor counter. The scent of cooking food wafted on the breeze, along with the far off scent of the ocean.

A young, fresh-faced waitress served her coffee and toast. With her peripheral vision Ema saw a figure slide into a seat next to her at the counter. The rest of the stools were unoccupied, and she wondered why he chose this place.

He ordered breakfast, and Ema pretended to ignore him, knowing he came for her. She reminded herself that Cole Deyo and Mickey Pinto knew her as Georgina, but she wondered if they remembered seeing her when she trailed after both women on New Year's Eve. She tensed, ready to react.

"Lady Sibyl?" the man asked in a low voice.

Ema turned and stared at him. Neither denying nor confirming the name he used, she continued to contemplate him in silence.

He was an older man, still handsome and broad across the shoulders. His handlebar mustache was white as was most of his thick hair. Crow's feet creased the sides of his blue eyes, and she sensed both intelligence and a sense of humor coming from him.

She finally raised an eyebrow and waited.

He studied her and realized he had been unprepared for how beautiful she was. A cloche hat covered most of her copper red hair. Dark lashes rimmed grayish green eyes with a sloe tilt to them. Full cupid lip, naturally tinted a dark pink offset her chiseled nose. A sun-kissed complexion burnished her cheekbones an apricot shade.

He'd been warned not to waste time with niceties and to come to the point quickly otherwise she would leave.

"Lady Sibyl, I need a bodyguard," he stated, "and they told me you would be the perfect person for this."

Ema masked her surprise very well, because there were few humans who knew her name.

"A bodyguard," she smiled, "who would recommend me as one?"

"Two men."

"What are their names?"

"Brother Miel."

The smile fled from Ema's face, and she tensed, leaning towards the man, tight as a bow. Throughout his life this man had been in many dangerous situations, but he couldn't recall ever experiencing the pervading sense of menace coming from one person.

"He's dead, has been for decades. Who's the other man?"

"Mort Peccatum."

Ema dropped her gaze and sat back in her seat. Her heart jumped, but her voice remained steady. "He's dead too. About ten years now."

"I know."

"That means only one thing."

"No, I don't belong to the Sempiterno Apostasy, but I am what they call one of the Dispossessed."

Ep Lentigo

Ephelis and Edward Lentigo, identical twin brothers were born March 3, 1863 in El Paso, Texas.

The summer of 1875, their family moved to Chicago, Illinois. Thereafter, both boys apprenticed out; Ephelis as a tanner, and Edward to a saddle shop. They continued in their schooling and Ephelis concentrated in civil engineering. Edward held no ambition to further his studies and held different jobs in the city.

This would not be the first time brothers, even twins, pursued different paths in their lives, but Mr. and Mrs. Lentigo recognized even so many years later, the shadow of what occurred to their sons when they were seven years old still held sway over them, especially Edward.

It was summer, and the boys decided to go exploring. They discovered an old cavern. It was after this that they experienced nightmares that escalated to a full-blown haunting that even their local priest did not understand how to stop. The boys saw figures they described as being demons; while other times they said humans that appeared to have met a grisly death communicated information about who murdered them.

At the ultimate moment of desperation, a friar arrived one winter day. Their parish priest introduced him as Brother Miel. He belonged to the mendicant order of San Hipólito. All the unnatural activity and noises stopped once he crossed the threshold of the abode.

He spent several days with the family and spoke to the boys. He blessed the house many times, and the activity ceased, but he urged them to move away from the area altogether when possible. While they called El Paso their home, they were never to allow the boys to return to the cavern they discovered.

It took five years for the family to gather enough funds to move to Chicago, and it was then they sensed all the shadows that lurked on the edges of their existence disappear. However, as parents they knew the effect on Edward was worse than with Ephelis.

The Lentigo brothers worked for the Great Western Railroad that ran from Chicago to Kansas City; Ephelis as a surveyor and Edward as a scout.

The brothers parted ways when Ephelis enlisted in the U.S. Army and as part of the Fourth United States cavalry was present when Geronimo and the Apache nation surrendered in 1886 at Skeleton Canyon, Arizona. His troop escorted the defeated Apaches to St. Augustine.

During those years stationed in the Southwest, Ephelis resurrected the memory of those dark days when he was seven years old. However he also learned how to chase smugglers, cattle thieves and fight other hostile Indian tribes.

He was honorably discharged from the army the winter of 1889 and promptly moved to Washington D.C. where his fiancée lived.

The year 1890 was a momentous one for him. He wed, became a father and joined the Metropolitan Police. During the decade that followed he ascended through the ranks, first as a sergeant and then he became a lieutenant. His life was blessed with plenty except a nagging sadness dogged him, because he had not heard from Edward for many years.

Everything changed in 1910. As a favor to a family friend he reopened an investigation into the disappearance of a governess by the name of Annabelle Smith. She worked for Dr. Levan Jackson, a prominent physician, and there was a question concerning a terse note she left behind saying she eloped with an unknown soldier to the west coast.

THE DEAD CAST NO SHADOW

Her family and a circle of close friends claimed this made little sense. She already had a sweetheart who was finishing law school. A few of them claimed that Annabelle hinted at strange going-ons with her employer, but she always stopped short of disclosing exactly what disturbed her. She depended on her job, since both her parents were ill, and her wedding was at least a year away.

Dr. Jackson postponed two meetings with him concerning the case, and one morning a detective came into his office with a solemn and troubled look on his face. His news drove all thought of the Smith case from his mind.

The man told him they discovered a body in a deserted part of the city. It was a man shot to death and left to rot in an empty warehouse. The stink of the putrefying remains led to its discovery. Lieutenant Lentigo, wondered why the detective seemed so hesitant in his description. The answer he received was not what he expected. It turned out the man looked identical to him.

Even before viewing the body, Ephelis feared it was Edward. It was this certitude that allowed the body's identification; otherwise he would have remained nameless. There were no clues found at the scene, no witnesses to be questioned; no suspects.

Ep never felt the separation from his brother more deeply than at this moment. He had nothing to offer as to the circumstances of his sibling's life, or even why he was in Washington D.C.

He didn't know if his brother had enemies, someone that settled a dispute by shooting him in the head. Edward had only twenty dollars in his wallet. His suit was expensive and well cut, nothing like what he wore the last time he saw him many years before. Then it was a clean but threadbare and well-used.

No leads developed, and the case grew cold despite the detective assigned to it giving it his full attention, since the victim was his brother.

Throughout the years Ephelis followed any hint of a clue, but they all came to naught.

Four years ago he retired from the police department, and two years later, his wife died. Their two sons had long ago established their lives and started a family. For the first time in many years, he had no responsibility towards anyone or anything and it was an unfamiliar circumstance that did not sit well with him.

Then last year the nightmares started. A gnarled, stringy-haired old man would beckon to him, but the waves of malevolence that came from the figure would awaken him in a cold sweat. One night he loosened his tongue and he asked the figure his name. It answered, "Levan Jackson."

The name brought him out of sleep. This was a person he had not thought of in years. He then realized the evil coming from the man, was the same he felt during those years in his childhood when hellish beings tortured Edward and him.

He wasn't sure when he decided that he would attempt to solve the mystery of what happened to his brother. He remembered those horrid days when the only person who understood the terribleness of what he saw was Edward, because he saw the same thing.

So many years later after the discovery of Edward's body, he found he was in the same position. He knew little or nothing about his brother. His life was a total mystery.

My Bodyguard

This was the story Ep Lentigo told the red-haired woman who listened to him with solemn eyes and interrupted once to ask him to call her Ema. He finished his story.

"How did your brother make money?" Ema asked him suddenly.

"He worked as a scout, but what's that saying about jack of all trades, master of none," he said. "Before I married, he would occasionally stay with me a spell, but he was a man of few needs, and then he would be off. When I asked him about his travels, he would have a funny story or an adventure to retell but there were some things he chose not to speak about."

Ep stopped a moment, and continued in a hoarse voice, "I never imagined the last time I saw him how ignorant I was about his life, and that he would be killed. If what you're asking is if he was a trouble maker, the answer is no, not the man I knew."

"You don't have to be a troublemaker for trouble to find you," Ema said.

"Yes," Lentigo said. "That was a lesson I learned early on as a policeman."

"When he told you his stories did he seem to always be in the same town?" Ema asked, as he took the first bite of his now lukewarm breakfast.

He chewed thoughtfully, and replied, "Not that I can recall, but I remember thinking he did a great deal of traveling, as far away as California."

"How about women or friends, did any of his stories involve the same person?" Ema asked.

41

"The impression I got was that he stayed nowhere long enough to develop these relationships."

"Do you think he would not tell you because he thought you would not approve?"

Ep Lentigo's eyes became moist, when he answered, "So many times, I've asked myself what the hell my brother was doing."

Ema stayed quiet for a moment, "Did he visit your parents through the years?"

"They saw him less than I did."

"Then what are you doing here in Miami, Mr. Lentigo?"

"My father died ten years ago, and my mother continued to stay in their house until she died five years ago. I kept the property shuttered, and a few months ago I traveled to Chicago and planned to sell it. I brought back a chest my mother used to gather family memorabilia."

Suddenly he stopped short, and Ema raised a questioning brow.

"Now that I think of it, this is when those nightmares started."

"What did you find in the chest?"

He cleared his throat and picked his words. "Among the letters and photographs, I found a postcard addressed to my brother dated after his death. On the reverse was a message that read, 'We are still here.' The return address is in this city, and it came from a woman named Joanne Goode."

"Let me guess this is when Brother Miel and Mort came to you?"

Ep looked at her in surprise, for she was so quick to accept the reality of their existence. It took him several days to realize they were not part of a random dream, and once he stopped resisting their message was clear. It was the tall man, who told him, "Use my name and she'll listen to you."

The ultimate test to prove that he was not losing his mind was to be at the place and time they indicated, and there she stood, or rather sat. However, even now, he didn't quite understand why they directed him to come and ask for her to guard him. In his world, men looked after women.

* * *

The Chevrolet Capitol truck came to a stop in front of a small bungalow shaded by coconut palms and overgrown foliage. Three shallow, limestone steps led to a screen porch, and the walls once whitewashed had paint flaking from them.

Ep banged on the screen door that clanked against its frame. The windows on either side were grimy and worn rattan furniture crowded a corner.

Ema waited at the sidewalk and noticed that most of the houses on the block had a shabby look.

A middle-aged woman wearing a pink and white uniform embroidered with the emblem of the Flamingo Hotel opened the door and stepped onto the porch. When she got a good look at Ep, she stumbled backwards almost losing her footing. She put a trembling hand over her mouth, and said, "Edward?"

"Are you Joanne?" Ep asked.

"It can't be," was her response.

"I'm not Edward, I'm his twin brother Ephelis." He stared at her through the dimness cast by the metal fabric between them.

From the murky interior came a woman's voice, "Momma, who is it?"

A young woman came up behind her mother. The dark hair and blue eyes proclaimed her as Edward Lentigo's child.

Flabbergasted, Ep finally found his voice, and said in a low voice, "Joanne, we need to speak."

The woman hesitated a moment, and opened the screen door. Ep turned around once and gestured for Ema to follow him.

43

Ep and Ema sat in a tidy but battered sofa and opposite to them Joanne and her daughter sat on two cushioned rattan chairs.

Ema introduced herself as Ep's assistant and then stayed silent.

Joanne held her head for a moment, tore her eyes upward and allowed herself to stare at Ep. She fought the truth that who sat before her was a stranger and not her child's father. The girl stared spellbound at Ep, knowing that she looked a great deal like him.

Ema sat next to Ep waiting for him to disclose what was apparent that this woman did not know, even if she suspected it.

"Edward is dead isn't he?" Joanne beat him to the revelation which he dreaded.

Ep cleared his throat. "Yes, he is."

The girl's eyes watered and she put her arm around the older woman's shoulder and hugged her.

"I knew it," she said. "I thought he abandoned us and that I didn't want to face the truth, but he would not do that. Even when he never returned or sent me word of where he was I still hoped he'd not turned his back on us."

Ep shook his head, "Joanne, my parents and me never were unaware you existed, otherwise we would have sought you out."

She asked the next logical question, "But why now, how did you find me?"

"The postcard you sent to my parent's address in Chicago. They are both deceased, and recently I went through their papers."

"I'd forgotten about that."

Ep looked at the young woman.

Joanne nodded, "Yes, this is Edward's daughter. Her name is Rachel."

"That was our mother's name."

There was silence in the room for a moment, and Joanne asked, "When did he die?"

THE DEAD CAST NO SHADOW

"A long time ago, in 1910, and all these years we never knew that Ed had a wife and child. I wish you'd sent him another letter, and my parent's would have found some solace in loving their granddaughter."

Joanne hung her head, and her cheeks flushed. Then she looked Ep straight in the eye. "We weren't married. It wouldn't have surprised me if Edward's family wanted nothing to do with us."

Ep looked at her blinking. He glanced over at Rachel who was staring at a distant point on the other side of the room.

"It would not have mattered to any of us," he responded.

Ema saw that Joanne tried to keep her composure. Her voice trembled when she said, "But, I guess it's too late for regrets. What's done is done."

"Joanne, I don't know many things about my brother's life in those years, but I knew my brother well enough that he would have done the honorable thing and married you especially if you were expecting his child."

"Perhaps he would have, if he was free to do so."

"What do you mean?" Ep's voice took on a somber tone.

"He couldn't marry me, because he was already another woman's husband."

It was Ephelis' turn to sit in shocked silence.

45

Those We Love Best

Joanne asked her daughter to go the corner drugstore and call her job at the hotel and explain she was sick and she would be there the following day.

Once Rachel left, Joanne turned to Ep and Ema. Her voice held no apology when she said, "I've told my daughter some things about her father, but not everything, and even now I want to protect her."

"I understand," said Ep. "For many years, my brother drifted in and out of my life, and I never pried because I believed he was entitled to his privacy even from me. You do not have to spare my feelings; I am ready to accept anything you have to say even if they are not complimentary of my brother's character."

"Very well," she responded. "Edward kept much of his past from me, including the fact he had a twin brother. So I will start when we met."

Joanne described how she had been hired as a maid at the home Edward shared with his wife Stella. It was a mansion with many servants. Married for many years, they led separate lives and he would be gone for months at a time. He took a nasty fall from a horse and was bedridden recuperating from the injuries. She would be the one to bring him trays of food and keep the room clean. He'd always been polite to her, and despite their age difference she thought he was a very handsome and kind man.

One day he asked her, "Mrs. Lentigo has left for the house on the coast?"

"Yes sir," she responded, "the summer heat has started."

She felt sorry for him. His wife never came to see him even though she lived inside the large house. She said something along those lines to him, and he responded, "Don't pity me, I am glad she's gone without me. As you can see our marriage is in name only."

During those days of summer he told her the story of how he traveled widely in the hunt for gold. He'd worked for different mining companies, scouting out areas for them, but he always sought places that had rumors of hidden treasure somewhere close by. He hinted that one day as a boy he'd found gold, but could not return to the place.

At the mention of this episode, Ep's face became taught and Ema sensed the tension that thrummed in his body, however he kept quiet and let Joanne continue.

Edward described how one time he'd invested in a mine that ruined him financially after a cave in.

The man he owed a great deal of money to approached him with a proposal to have the debt forgiven in its entirety. All he had to do was marry his daughter.

There was a great deal of scandal attached to her. She'd been married, and for many years there was no child. Convinced the fault lay with her husband, she ran off with a lover, only to find she didn't conceive a child with him either. The truth was she was a barren woman. The lover abandoned her, and the cuckolded husband cast her away in a scandalous divorce because of her adultery.

Edward told her, "So you see Joanne, they have bought me like the cattle my father-in-law owns. All he wanted was to minimize the damage that his daughter's conduct cast on him and his good name. A new husband meant she wasn't entirely ruined. We wed in a private ceremony, and he built this house far from society and anyone who could remember what she'd done."

He'd been quiet for a moment, and then said, "She doesn't love me, and the sad truth is I have no love for her either. I have my freedom, but only at the end of a leash."

Joanne's face softened with memories. "We fell in love. When his wife returned after being gone the entire summer, she noticed something different about him. Perhaps the other servants whispered what they suspected, and it reached her ears. Within days of her arrival they fired me. Edward found a place for me to live, and told me he planned to divorce her, but he needed money to free us from the influence of his wife and her father."

Her face became set. "He returned after a few days and he was a changed man. He urged me to pack all our belongings and we left the next day. He was worried and frightened. He told me we were heading to Florida; that he'd heard stories about a lost treasure in the Everglades."

She sighed and continued, "I'd follow him to the end of the world. They raised me in an orphanage which is how I got the job at their home. There was nothing for me in Texas. I told him I suspected I would have a baby. He was so happy, but also worried. Edward bought this little house for us and promised me that soon he would have us living in a spacious home for our child to grow up in. He told me he had to leave for a few days and left the address in Chicago and a small amount of money. I never saw him again."

Rachel's steps sounded on the steps, and then the screen door clanked. Joanne wiped tears away from her cheek, and smiled wanly.

Ep unclenched his fists and watched the blood flow back into his fingers.

He asked, "Joanne, who was his father-in-law?"

She faltered a moment, "Senator Gordon."

"Senator Gordon from Texas?" Ep's voice was subdued.

"Yes."

"Where did Edward live with his wife?"

"El Paso," was her answer.

"He never mentioned he lived there until he was twelve years old?"

"No," her shocked expression spoke volumes, "once I tried to ask him about his childhood, and I think that was one of the few times he grew angry with me, and told me never to ask him about that again."

All That I Am

Sergeant Getty stood in the Halcyon Hotel manager's office.
They waited for the concierge to join them. He was there
investigating the death of two women. One appeared to have taken
a swan dive out an open window on the fifth floor, however
another sustained severe injuries to her body that would have
resulted in immediate death. But there was no blood around her
corpse or any sign they had beaten her inside the room.

Mr. Pierce, the concierge nervously entered the office.

Sergeant Getty told the manager he would speak to his
employee alone, and with a hesitant step he left his own office. His
only concern was safeguarding the reputation of the hotel, and he
glowered meaningfully at his employee.

The policeman came quickly to the point. He asked, "Mr. Pierce,
who are these women?"

The concierge weighed his options. It was evident the police
called him because someone already whispered to the sergeant of
his involvement. As a precaution, told the truth, but omitted certain
facts.

"I was told they were two nurses involved in a serious accident
on the way to Miami."

"Were they traveling on the Tamiami Trail?"

"I believe so."

"The Halcyon I would think would be a little too pricey for
nurses." Sergeant Getty stayed quiet, waiting for Pierce to explain
how they became guests there.

"Their stay was paid for."

"By whom?"

"One man they were traveling with wanted to make sure they had a safe place to stay until their return to St. Petersburg."

"What's his name?"

"Cole Deyo."

Sergeant Getty was well acquainted with Mr. Deyo. He was a small-time bootlegger who operated out of a onetime bakery, with a speakeasy on the second floor. After the hurricane of 1926, the business closed, and the building stood shuttered. He suspected the liquor stored on the second floor would later be distributed around town and to the Florida's west coast by Cole.

"Anyone else?" the sergeant queried.

"Only he came in with them." Pierce didn't mention that Mickey Pinto waited out in the automobile.

Getty suspected that Deyo got a special rate for their room; otherwise he would have dropped the women off at a flop house on the outskirts of town.

"How 'bout their names?"

"No."

"You mean you received two guests without having them register at your front desk? Isn't that unusual?"

Pierce swallowed to clear his dry throat. "Mr. Deyo explained they were involved in a serious accident where they all barely escaped with their lives. He left money for a meal, a change of clothing and their stay. I thought it a Christian act of charity to allow them a place to stay."

"They were here more than one day."

"Yes, one of them came down yesterday and paid for two extra nights."

"Did you get her name at that point?"

"No." Mr. Pierce felt the beads of sweat pop out on his forehead.

"Which of the two paid for those days?"

"The dark-haired one."

"Was there anything unusual about them, anything to indicate one would end up dead in her room, and the other on the sidewalk outside the Halcyon?"

"No."

The policeman shut the small notebook he wrote in. He had already spoken to the hotel operator who told him the blonde one asked to be connected to Faith Hospital in St. Petersburg.

"That's all for now Mr. Pierce, if you recall any other information please contact me." Sergeant Getty glared at him with weary eyes.

"Of course, of course." The rotund, middle-age man fought the urge to loosen his tie, and hastily left the room.

* * *

Ema and Ep sat in the small living room sipping coffee Joanne prepared for them. Ep realized that so much had been disclosed in a short amount of time, that perhaps it was better to give them time to digest it, so the talk changed to lighter subjects.

Suddenly a hard scrabbling noise sounded over their heads. They all looked at one another, and Ema saw at once that it mystified both women.

Joanne spoke up, "There's only a crawl space above us."

Someone laughed, but it sounded like a small child, high-pitched and shrill.

Joanne remembered those first months she spent in the house alone when strange noises would awaken her. Alone and pregnant she became close to an older woman, named Mary who was a next-door neighbor. Later she helped care for Rachel, and once they became better acquainted, Joanne confided about the strange noises she would hear every few weeks coming from the narrow space between the ceiling and the roof of the house.

THE DEAD CAST NO SHADOW

Mary told her that prior to her occupancy of the house it stood empty for many years. Once it was being cleaned out for new tenants, they discovered a small boy's mummified remains in the narrow attic space. None remembered a child ever living there, but the neighbors changed over the years.

Many years before, the houses on the block were built for laborers coming in from the Caribbean who worked at different construction sites.

The old woman came over with her Bible one evening and prayed out loud as she walked through the small home. She placed a crucifix over the narrow door to the space, and the noise ceased, until this moment.

Ema stood up, and for once all the others gathered there realized she was present.

"Where's the entry to that space?" she asked Joanne.

"In the hallway between the two bedrooms."

A rotting odor, so foul that it stung their nostrils filled the small living room.

Ema walked towards the area that Joanne indicated. She shook her head at Ep who made to stand up and follow her. Across from the bedrooms, the doorway to the bathroom stood open. It drew her eyes to a movement behind a shower curtain that surrounded a claw-foot tub.

The stink increased as she stepped closer and the curtain fluttered. With her finger she pulled the cloth back and saw what looked like a naked boy with its back to her. The arms were crossed over its knees, and his head tucked down. Grime covered the thin almost skeletal frame.

The child turned to look at her over its shoulder and it screamed. It was a poor imitation of a human boy, and the empty sockets glittered with small, obsidian bits. Only nasal bones above a

53

mouthful of narrow, jagged teeth completed the face of a bedeviled corpse. It hissed at Ema.

She sensed movement behind her and saw that Ep looked over her shoulder. She heard the sharp intake of his breath and he stumbled backwards stifling a yell.

The thing hissed again, and scrabbled up the tub onto a cramped ledge below an open window overlooking the jungly back yard of the home. It kicked the screen outwards and on all fours launched the skinny body into the thick, shrubbery below and disappeared.

Ema turned back and looked at his blanched face. Her voice was low and steady when she said, "That's why Brother Miel wanted me to guard your back."

Dagger in the Heart

"Expect it will get worse," Ema said matter-of-factly.

Ephelis Lentigo felt like his innards were being squeezed. He leaned heavily against the pink and black tiled wall behind him. In an instant the sensation transported him back over fifty years to the dark days when he was seven years old.

"Why worse?" he croaked.

"Because now it's knows you are not alone."

Ema turned and walked back towards where both women waited for them. Their faces where tense with fright, and they dared not move from the chairs where they sat. From their vantage point they did not see what was in the bathroom, only heard the scuffle.

Ep collected himself and followed Ema back to the living room. The odor still floated around them, with an acrid bitter edge laced with remnants of sulfur.

She directed her question to Joanne, "You suspect the origins of this?"

The woman nodded silently.

"Tell us," Ema instructed.

Joanne described the events she experienced the first months she lived in the home, and how Mary who died many years ago had been her salvation.

Rachel's pretty face pinched with concern when she heard how her mother endured this torment in her solitude.

"Joanne, this is not the spirit of a child, it's the evil betrayal committed against him."

"But why, after so many years is this happening?"

"That's a good question, but we are here to protect you."

Both women nodded, afraid to ask how. They were just glad that someone combated something they had little or no understanding of.

Ema turned to Ep, "I'll wait for you outside." She turned to Joanne and Rachel, "It was a pleasure to meet you."

The pair murmured their goodbyes.

Ema stood at the sidewalk under the shade cast by the fronds of two coconut palms. The noon sun shone down from a cloudless, blue sky. She opened her right hand palm up and captured a ray of sunlight that shimmered and took the shape of a dancing cube.

She said only one word, "*Sepio*." The sunbeam quivered and darted into the underbrush surrounding the small property.

Ep left the house and came to open the door of the truck for Ema. He started the vehicle. When they reached the end of the block, he stopped and turned to the red-haired woman sitting next to him. "Who are you?" he asked her.

"The answer is simple, but complex at the same time. I think you'll understand better in the coming days."

He stared at her a moment, then nodded.

After traveling in silence for a few minutes, he turned to her, "Where are you staying?"

"Until earlier today at the Halcyon Hotel."

He cleared his throat, and continued, "Well allow me to get us each a room there. Ema, I wasn't sure what I would find when I got here, but not this. Amid this insanity I've discovered I have a niece. But I have so many unanswered questions."

"Perhaps you are at the right place to find answers." They reached an intersection, and she said, "Leave me off at a dress shop close to the hotel, and hold my room under the name of E. St George."

The rest of the short ride continued in silence. Ep for a moment allowed himself to enjoy the weather which hovered around seventy degrees. He remembered the rest of the United States was enduring frigid temperatures.

Ema pointed out a small shop and before she stepped away she said, "Make sure our rooms are close together. If they cannot give us a room on the same floor, then do not take them and wait for me in the lobby."

Ep nodded, the policeman in him recognizing the wisdom of her recommendation. He recognized everything was connected; the series of weird dreams, the decision to search for his brother's murderer and an encounter with a creature that was the stuff of his childhood nightmares. It did not escape his attention that whatever hid in the tub, ran away from Ema. Did she belong to the Sempiterno Apostasy? Perhaps, but he suspected there was more to this woman than this.

When Ep walked up the steps leading into the hotel, someone called out his name. He turned and saw a tall man with a broad smile approaching. It took him a moment to recognize Eli Getty who once worked in Washington D.C.'s police force, but that had been ten years before. He moved to Miami for his wife's health and taken a job with the local police department.

"Lieutenant Lentigo, what are you doing here?"

They shook hands heartily.

Ep already practiced a story to explain his presence.

"I'm not a lieutenant any more. Retired, and I came to enjoy the weather. I'm thinking of writing my memoirs. Making up for all those vacations I never took."

"And your family?" Sergeant Getty asked.

"My sons are well, but I lost my wife a few years ago."

"I'm sorry to hear this."

They exchanged pleasantries and traded stories about their experiences on the police force.

Across the street, Cole Deyo and Mickey Pinto watched the two men talking. Word had reached them of what happened to May and Georgina, and they came ready to get the story from Pierce. The concierge already sent them a message that Getty was pressing him about why he'd allowed the women to stay without having them register. They suspected foul play.

Mickey relayed May's conversation to Cole about Georgina's repentance.

"I knew that dame was bad news." Cole murmured.

"Who?" Mickey asked.

"Georgina."

"It was your idea to bring them to Miami." Mickey pointed out.

"Yeah, don't remind me, but after that accident, there was something off about her."

"So who do you think is that big guy talking to Getty? Could he be Georgina's uncle?"

"He's got copper written all over him, and I've heard they pull some of these old sons-of-bitches out of retirement and make them G-men."

"I wonder if she got to tell him anything."

"Who knows, but if he's the uncle, he got here mighty quick. We'll keep an eye out, and pick up Pierce when he leaves to go home, and get the story from him."

Both men stayed quiet when they saw a tall woman walk up to the conversing men. The cloche hat partially hid her face, but her beauty was obvious.

Mickey whistled low, "Will you look at that."

"Yeah, I am, but we need to steer clear of this place for a while. Last thing we need is to get questioned about a murder. Remember tonight we've also got a shipment that we need to bring up the river."

THE DEAD CAST NO SHADOW

Suddenly the woman turned her head and looked directly at both men parked across the street. It was not a causal glance but direct eye contact that took them in individually. There was no doubt she was observing and remembering their faces.

"Do you know her?" Mickey asked in a low voice.

"No, I don't, and I would remember if I did."

"Well, she's looking at us like she knows who we are."

Cole Deyo could not deny the unsettled feeling that sank in his belly, and he hastily drove off, unwilling to deal with the fact that he wanted to escape her gaze.

Ema introduced herself as Ep's secretary and stenographer who helped him prepare his book. She guessed that Eli Getty wondered if this was a truthful statement, but was wise enough to realize it was none of his business.

Several minutes later, the conversation ended and Ep asked for two rooms at the front desk. The manager watched him conversing with Sergeant Getty on the steps outside and decided against probing deeper about the red-haired woman. He recognized poise in her that did not fit with a woman of low standing, on the contrary she could put many New York socialites to shame.

Ema waited by a potted palm in the lobby and watched May's ghost mill about among the guests. She'd feared this would happen when the tormented woman ended her life so abruptly. She did not realize that she'd been successful, and failed to understand why no one interacted with her. Eventually she would return to the room and reenact her suicide, the last few moments absent from her memory.

Ep came up to Ema and handed her a key. "They gave us adjoining rooms. As you asked, I told them to take the delivery from the dress shop to your room."

A bellboy retrieved Ep's bags from his truck and they walked to the elevator which clanged as its door opened. Ep's body stiffened,

59

and he stopped in his tracks. Ema looked around him and saw May waiting inside. Part of her skull split open, with her blood and brains staining the white nightgown she wore.

Ema whispered to him, "I can see her also; only we can. She cannot do anything to you."

Ep followed the bellboy woodenly into the elevator, but the ride was short since their rooms were on the second floor. As the group moved away, they overheard the young woman operating the controls complain when it continued upwards instead of back to the lobby. Unbeknownst to her, she carried a passenger who held an appointment with destiny on the fifth floor which could not be ignored.

Within a few minutes, Ep knocked at the door between their rooms. When he faced Ema his features were still etched with fear.

She forestalled him and asked, "Ep, you've seen the dead before, haven't you?"

"Yes, but after childhood, only shadows or an occasional whisper which I ignored. Not like this. I don't understand why now."

"Do you know who she was?"

"No," he stated quietly.

"She committed suicide early this morning by leaping from the fifth floor of this hotel. Her name is May Jackson, her father was Levan Jackson."

Seconds of silence stretched between them.

"I have not heard that name in many years." He stopped, "No I am mistaken, when these nightmares started an old man appeared to me, and said he was Levan Jackson."

"Coincidence;" Ema asked. "why would he come to you?"

"It's been almost twenty years ago, that I investigated the disappearance of his employee Annabelle Smith. This was unlike her, but we found no evidence of foul play. Apart from this I had nothing to do with him."

"Did you believe she ran away with a man who she knew her family and friends would not approve of?" Ema asked.

"Yes, we suspected this based on a note she left behind. She'd been working for Jackson for about five years, and for the last year before her disappearance she mentioned to her friends there was something about his behavior that disturbed her. When they pressed her for clarification she would change the subject, however without specifics what could they do against a man with a solid reputation in the community, and peers who would vouch for his character?"

"What became of your investigation? Did she ever write again to her parents, friends or even her fiancée?" Ema knew the answer to this question, but she understood this man needed to be led to uncomfortable conclusions about what was unfolding around him.

"No, the last time I inquired they'd not even received a postcard from her. When they killed Edward, I had just begun my efforts in her case. I spared no thought for a poor governess who for all I knew was alive and well with her lover."

Ep turned and trudged back into his room. He sat down, sighed and rubbed his forehead. Then he looked up at Ema with eyes full of sorrow. He said, "For years I thought Edward came to Washington D.C. looking for me. Now I find out that his father-in-law was one of the most powerful politicians in the country. What if this was all about Senator Gordon?"

Ema asked, "Was your brother's murder ever publicized at all?"

"No," he replied, "I took pains to keep it out of the newspapers. I didn't want any scandal attached to him, or to cause my parents distress. Stories like this interfere with an investigation instead of helping. Newspapermen wanted to stay on my good side and thought it was a robbery that ended in a tragedy. It didn't take much convincing for them to forget the story."

Ema returned his stare and asked, "Perhaps your brother was there to see both you and his father-in-law. You're the policeman Ephelis, do you think there's a connection between everything?"

"Undoubtedly, and I'll be damned if I don't figure this out, once and for all."

Ema's next words were unexpected, "I will help you with one mystery, which I doubt you would ever solve."

Ep stood up again, "What is it?"

"Levan Jackson had a hand in Annabelle Smith's murder. He paid someone to get rid of her. I am sure he fabricated the note she left behind."

"How would you know this?" he asked immediately.

Ema reminded herself that Ep existed in a world of evidence and facts, despite his brush with the supernatural world.

"You could say I got it straight from the horse's mouth, but Ep I am speaking the truth. I am sure that if you investigated you would find that Levan Jackson died only a few months ago, about the time you saw him in your dreams."

Ep's eyes searched her face, and her words rang with undeniable conviction. He said, "It seemed as if the earth swallowed her. Without evidence of foul play, or even a body there was nothing to disprove she did not leave of her own free will. There was no reason to disbelieve her note."

"Were you aware that Levan Jackson apprenticed to an undertaker before entering medical school?"

"No." he replied. Ema followed his train of thoughts. If there was a trade which knew how to get rid of a body without leaving behind a clue, it would be an undertaker.

He continued, "My next question would be why, but if she discovered something damaging about good Dr. Jackson while living under his roof, well let's say I've seen many murders committed for less reason than this."

"Which brings us to now," Ema spoke softly. "You've traveled to a city in search of news about your dead brother and find more than you expected. You came to stay in a hotel where only a few hours ago Dr. Levan's daughter leapt to her death. You are meant to be here, and even if you've chosen to ignore the dead in the past, they feel differently."

Ephelis Lentigo nodded in agreement.

Ema returned to her room. She did not share with him that more than the dead were hovering around them, creatures much more dangerous circled on the periphery.

She swept a tear away from her eye. How could she explain the longing that filled her heart to hear Mort's name again and know that her avatar hunted with her from the land of the dead? She admitted to herself and herself alone, that she still mourned him bitterly even after so many years.

Watcher in the Shadows

She stood across the street in the shadow of the empty house.
Throughout the day, she'd been hiding in a dark and damp crawl
space underneath the structure awaiting the sunset. A porch light
shone like a lonely firefly at the place she watched now.

The older woman came out to water several rose bushes. She
stopped and became still as if listening for a sound that escaped
her. The watcher crouched lower into soil crawling with vermin
and discarded trash from the prior occupants of the home. Her
attention was riveted to the woman, who resumed her mundane
activity. A few minutes later she finished her task, and headed back
inside. A yellow light from a lamp lit up the windows.

She wanted to come closer and peer inside, so she could see the
younger one and fill her nostrils with her scent, but she dared not.
She sensed the small guardian that circled unseen through the
property.

That did not worry her that much, however whoever loosed it
there did, so for now she would content herself with watching and
waiting for the right moment to strike.

* * *

John Cheney, carpenter and alcoholic, ambled down the quiet
and empty city block. He'd come here because many of the houses
were unoccupied, and January nights in Miami turned nippy after
the midnight hour. Overhead palm fronds rustled in the nighttime
air, and far off a dog barked.

He stopped in front of a small bungalow with a sagging porch.
His bleary eyes assessed it, and he nodded to no one in particular

64

his approval. He tottered drunkenly through the yellow weeds that choked the walkway. A smelly cloud of stale sweat followed in his wake. His steps sounded hollowly on the planks of the entrance. He reached behind a potted plant where he stuffed some rags he used previously as a pillow.

John sank to the floor and pulled his ratty coat collar tighter around his neck. He smiled to himself thinking this was much better than a cardboard box in a derelict alley. Within minutes his rough snore filled the silence.

He'd ridden the rails into Miami in 1926, two months before a hurricane punished the city unmercifully. It devastated the area, but a master carpenter found a wealth of opportunity for those seeking to rebuild. However those who gave him work, soon found out why such a talented artisan was a hobo. He was a drunkard, and he cared not a whit there were laws prohibiting alcohol consumption.

He only got jobs that would take one day to complete, and they supervised him closely to make sure he didn't take a drink. This was the way he survived since then.

From deep in the cavern of his memory, before liquor consumed everything good in his life, he recalled the smoothness of his young wife's body in his arms. During chilly nights when icy winds and snow pelted the window he would reach out and bring her close. She would nuzzle his shoulder and curve her body into his.

He sensed her now, her fiery breath against his neck, and long legs draped across his thigh. A sandpapery tongue stroked his skin; rough like a cat's. And she continued to lick, as when an animal is savoring the taste of a favorite food.

A pleasant numbing flooded over him, while another part of his brain sounded an alarm for him to awaken. The hot exhalation trailed down his throat past his sternum and settled on his stomach. The rough tonguing continued, and the enjoyment receded as the pressure built, and a throb of pain shot through the rest of body.

A foul-smelling hand covered his mouth and nostrils with an irresistible pressure, and sharp teeth took the first bite of his belly. His scream was buried behind what covered his face, and he tried to move his limbs, but a heavyweight pinned him down. His prematurely aged body did not have the strength to cast it off.

He opened his eyes and saw the top of something's head slowly teasing his innards out, and there was not sufficient alcohol in his system to anesthetize the pain of being eaten alive.

Death did not claim him when the creature champed into his shoulder and dragged him underneath the house. He was still conscious when he heard it dig a shallow hole. It bit him once more and pulled him into the pit. Like a cat burying its feces she threw dirt on top of him and lay on her prize. Later she would continue feasting.

John Cheney died in agony and asphyxiated, in ignorance of what attacked him. All he knew was that it was not of this world.

The Unmarked Grave

Winter dusk came early, and Ema and Ep stepped into the narrow elevator. They headed to a nearby hotel where a Chinese restaurant gained a superior reputation for their food.

A young man operating the controls slid back the door, and a flash of powder from a camera blinded them for a moment. A man who identified himself as a reporter from the local newspaper stepped forward blocking their way.

"Lieutenant Lentigo, is it true you're here from Washington to help with the bootleggers flaunting the laws of the country?"

For a moment Ep stayed silent, unprepared for this encounter. He answered in a steady voice, "No, I am retired, and I am not here in any law enforcement capacity on behalf of any department. Please step aside."

He guided Ema by the elbow and pushed the man aside.

Undaunted the man followed behind him. "Why are you here?"

"For the same reason all the other visitors come, for the glorious weather."

"Are you saying the rumor that you're now a G-Man pulled out of retirement is untrue?"

"Yes."

Ep continued to guide Ema towards the front door, and other guests who milled in the lobby looked on with curious eyes.

Many murmured amongst themselves, wondering who the woman accompanying the tall man was. She wore a dark gown with a fur edged coat, black pumps and a felt hat of the same color that caused her red curls to stand out. The style was minimal but looked very chic, and many tried to guess if she was a Washington socialite traveling incognito.

The reporter and his photographer followed them to where a taxicab waited. They seated themselves and the door slammed behind them when Ema stared at the young man holding the camera. Unexpectedly it danced out of his grasp, falling to the floor and shattering in numerous pieces. The photograph was ruined.

Ep told the driver their destination and sat back with a grunt. "That was unexpected."

Ema reminded him, "This hotel made the newspapers when two women staying as their guests ended up dead. They need a story to draw attention away from that scandal."

"Well, I'd wish they'd chosen another patron for that purpose."

The ride to the restaurant was short, and Ep asked for a table in a secluded area. They placed their order, and as soon as the waiter walked away, Ep declared, "You were right."

"I was, about what?"

"Levan Jackson. I made some phone calls, and they confirmed his death a few months ago. To think this man died in squalor. He lost his fortune and stature as a medical doctor many years ago."

"Some life choices are more unwise than others." Ema said mysteriously.

"I spent most of last night trying to remember more about Annabelle Smith's case, and a conversation that I did not pay much attention to at the time came to mind."

"And what was the conversation about?" Ema asked.

"The detective handling it believed she was an unhappy young lady who ran off, so he'd not put much effort into scrutinizing it. I did it as a favor to friends of the family. Well I was attending a dinner party, and I ended up speaking to a retired captain from the Metropolitan police. We were talking about recent interesting cases and I mentioned the request by Annabelle's relatives."

"May I anticipate a little about your story at this point?"

"Yes of course."

"You mentioned the name of Levan Jackson."

Ep's eyebrows lifted in surprise. "Yes, I did."

"Please continue."

"The captain's demeanor changed drastically. He warned me to be discreet when following this lead. He alluded to resistance coming from the university, and even some political figures in the government."

"I told him I would not ruin a man's reputation over unproven allegations, and I was sure Dr. Jackson had connections with players in the Washington circuit. He told me something that perplexed me at the moment, but now I understand was a clear warning. He said, 'Lentigo, it's not false accusations that raise the most outcries, but the ones close to the truth. Unless you come upon indisputable evidence about this being a murder, then set it aside for your family's sake. If she's alive, she'll resurface. If she's dead and lying in an unmarked grave, let her lie there.' He changed the subject and never asked me about the case again."

"This was before your brother's murder?"

"Yes." Ep stayed quiet, staring into Ema's eyes. Her question was not a simple inquiry, and his stomach tightened him when he followed where that question would lead.

She broke into his reverie. "Did you know the two women found dead at the Halcyon came to Miami in the company of bootleggers?"

"No. Ema I worry every time you ask me a question."

"That's not my intention. I am guarding you by making you aware of these facts."

"So, that newspaper reporter, was in reality doing a favor for some Miami gangster who's trying to find out if I'm working for Hoover?"

69

"Possibly, but I'm pointing it out because your stay in Miami, whatever your personal reasons, might be interpreted a different way."

Ep leaned back in his chair and took a sip of his drink. "That's all I need, rum-runners suspecting I'm here to bust up their action."

Ema shrugged her shoulders and smiled at him.

Ep leaned forward and asked, "So, when will you tell me a little more about you Ema? We met only this morning, and I know nothing, but you know everything about me."

Ema considered her answer, and replied, "I'm not important; rest assured I am here to help you. Perhaps in the coming days you'll have more of an answer to your question."

Ep realized he would have to be content with her response. All his instincts as a policeman told him she was an invaluable ally, so he did not press her for clarification.

During the rest of the meal Ep told Ema about his family and his career in the police department. He was a wonderful storyteller, and time slipped away pleasantly.

Once outside, they waited at the curb while a doorman hailed a taxi for them. Two towering statues of fu dogs graced the imposing doors of the restaurant, their mouths opened in an eternal grimace.

Ema saw Ep blink rapidly and stare at one sculpture. She turned and saw what made him stared fixedly at the images. The eyes of the male figurine blinked. The enormous orbs, now shiny were looking back at him. As guardians they were placed at the entrance, and something caused them to be activated. At that moment a taxi pulled up, and she caught Ep by the arm and pulled him into the interior. He did not resist her and slid into the seat. She looked at the female sculpture which also became animated.

Shocked into silence, Ep sat mute next to her and she directed the driver to the Halcyon.

He turned to her, "Tell me you saw it too."

THE DEAD CAST NO SHADOW

She nodded and became concerned it would overwhelm him. These events stripped away the blinders he kept in place for so many years. She suspected this was an effort to drive him towards insanity.

Her eyes locked with the driver's, which were looking at her through the rearview mirror. In an instant she saw the irises inside the green pupils lengthen and become inhuman. The shoulder seams of his coat ripped as the body it covered enlarged beyond their original fit.

Ema lunged over the seat, as a shrill scream echoed inside the confines of the auto, and it sounded like something that came not from a human throat. The car swerved as she pulled the struggling, howling thing into the back seat, and she yelled only one word at Ep, "Drive!"

The adrenaline rush that he experienced only moments before when he witnessed inanimate objects come to life, propelled him forward without thinking to question what was happening. He grabbed at the wheel, as the feet of the driver kicked inches from his face.

Ema pulled the struggling creature into the back seat while beating it about the face. Large canines dominated its features when the lips curled back and it resembled an angry baboon.

In those seconds Ep didn't question how he pulled his bulky frame into the driver's seat, all he knew was that he found himself there; the growling and jostling behind him attesting to the ferocity of the fight. He swerved the car over a curb onto a deserted sidewalk and stopped it. Ep scrambled out and pulled the door open, his heart thudding in his chest, expecting to see Ema dead.

Instead her sweaty face stared back at him as she laid full length on something that he tried desperately to fit into his understanding of reality. Strands of her copper hair draped in damp disarray

71

across her forehead. The figure underneath her made no movement.

Ep caught her up by her under her armpits and dragged her out, inspecting her as he did for any signs of injury, but except for tears in her dress he saw none.

His hands trembled as he held her at arm's length and inspected her once more. Then he saw why the creature lay still. The pommel of a wicked looking dagger stuck out from under its chin. She buried it to the hilt. Fur surrounded an almost simian face, and its fingers ended in curved talons.

"What is it?" he asked, in a steady voice it surprised him to hear come from his own throat.

"A mimic demon," she answered matter-of-factly. "It can only hold a disguise for a certain amount of time, but it can resemble any creature including humans."

Ep looked around and saw they arrived in a deserted street where construction sites lined the lonely avenue. No doubt it brought them here precisely because of this.

"What now?"

In response, Ema stepped forward and pulled out the dagger. It shimmered and sparkled in her hand, and it surprised him when she stuck it into her abdomen as if she held a sheath in her body.

"Its name is Iron Horse, and I kept it handy since we left the hotel. I'm not hurting myself placing it there." She read the concern in his face, and he turned and followed her gaze. The demon's form smoked and the faint sound of sizzling preceded a horrible odor of decay as it consumed itself into dust.

She reached into the seat and retrieved her purse.

"We need to leave this area now," she stated in a low voice.

He looked around with practiced eyes and saw that they were the only ones there, but it was only a matter of time before someone came upon them.

THE DEAD CAST NO SHADOW

They crossed the street, and he realized they were one block over from the hotel.

Ema spoke to him as they walked in the shadow of a looming structure under construction. "Tomorrow they will find the body of the original driver somewhere close to the restaurant, and then the car."

Once they reached the corner opposite the hotel, he was about to shrug out of his jacket to cover her ripped dress, when she shook her head. "Do not worry, I will cast a momentary glamour where I will be seen but overlooked, is the best way to describe it. No one will notice, head straight to the elevator."

Ep nodded and understood any questions he wanted to ask would have to wait.

What few persons were in the lobby failed to react to them, and as they came to the intricately carved door of the elevator, it slid open.

Out stepped a middle-aged man with silvered, shoulder length hair and a full beard. Powerfully built, and he made the hotel uniform look regal.

"Sibyllina, always the troublemaker." He tsked, tsked as he clanged the gate close, and the conveyor lurched upwards. Ema stared ahead, ignoring him.

Ep looked at the man and then at Ema.

The elevator operator turned his twinkling blue eyes to Ep. "Please order her a new outfit, she goes through clothing at an alarming rate."

Ep nodded in agreement.

The lift bumped to a stop, and the man opened the door on the second floor. Once they stepped out, he closed it and the gears grinded as it returned to the lobby.

Ep pulled Ema into his room, unwilling to let her out of his sight.

"Asking who that was is the last question I have about everything that happened tonight."

Ema sat down and kicked her shoes off, stretching out her toes. She looked up at Ep who stood silent and waiting.

"I have my own questions," she said.

"You do?"

"Who was the creature here for; you or me?"

"And to think I was worried about suspicious bootleggers," Ephelis remarked.

Blood is Thicker Than Water

The door between the two rooms stood ajar. The cool weather allowed windows to be left open to catch the breeze coming in from Biscayne Bay. There was no need for mosquito netting. The night was profound and silent those last hours before dawn, so Ema heard Ep scream hoarsely in a mixture of fear and heartbreak.

Preferring always to err on the side of caution she held her sword Zeruko Neskamea within the folds of her long muslin nightgown as she crept into Ep's room. In the oblique shadows it winked with its own golden light once her hand gripped the pommel crowned with a pink diamond.

Ema stood outside the parted door and stared at Ep thrashing violently amid the blankets of his bed. A nightmare held him in its grip.

She came to his side and shook him. He opened his eyes and stared at her with eyes full of fright and without recognition. All he saw was a beautiful woman, with long red hair, holding a wicked looking sword. His features relaxed, and he said, "Ema."

"What were you dreaming?"

"Eddie came to me, and I saw him the way he looked when they discovered his corpse. His bloated body lay there, and the sorrow of his death was as fresh as the moment I first knew about it. Then he was next to me, and somehow he was trying for me to see him how he appeared when he was alive, and he achieved it. I realized in that moment that something was trying to impede him from reaching out to me. Right before you woke me, he mouthed one word, and it was 'Rachel'."

Ema stayed silent. She looked at Ep's face, and the dark circles forming under his eyes. He needed to sleep. There would be time

75

enough tomorrow to speak of what this dream meant. She reached out and placed her forefinger between his eyes, and said the word, "Sleep."

His eyelids drooped, and he slumped over into his pillow. She covered him and returned to her room.

* * *

Ep slept late into the morning. Ema ordered room service, and she sat sipping coffee when he emerged, hair tousled but his face rested.

"Come and eat," she said.

He finished tying his robe around him and sat next to her.

"So where is it?" he asked.

"It?"

"The sword you came into my room with last night."

Ema smiled at him and said, "A story for another day."

After he served himself breakfast from the covered tray, he asked her, "Eddie came to me last night. It was not a nightmare. He is worried for his daughter."

"Do you remember the question I asked about last night?"

"Yes."

"Perhaps that mimic demon came for both of us."

He stopped chewing and listened to her with undivided attention.

"It came for me because I'm guarding you, and it came for you because… "

Ep gulped his food down, and finished the sentence, "Because my brother wants me to guard his daughter."

"I believe so. The question is why she would become important after existing in relative obscurity all her life. She doesn't have your surname, you didn't even know about her until yesterday."

"Why would my family matter to these hellish creatures?"

"That is what we need to find out Ep."

"How much danger are Rachel and her mother in?" He asked earnestly.

"Considerable danger Ep, which is why we need to figure out what part of this puzzle is missing."

Ema poured herself another cup of coffee, then asked, "Ep when you started working on Annabelle's case, did you ask anyone in particular to look into Dr. Jackson on your behalf?"

"I brought in the detective that first handled the case, hoping I could find something he overlooked. But Ema I thought we would find Miss Smith alive and well, living somewhere on the west coast."

"What did you ask the detective about concerning the good doctor?"

"When I reviewed his notes, I found he didn't speak to Jackson at all, and only relied on one interview with the housekeeper who spoke glowingly of her employer. The woman even stressed that she wasn't surprised Annabelle Smith ran off."

"Did he explain why he did not speak to Dr. Jackson?"

"Come to think of it, he became quite upset when I told him I wanted him to return and question Jackson about the allegations. However, I was his superior, and he knew I expected him to close out the case to my satisfaction."

"How soon after this was your brother murdered?"

A sudden stillness descended upon Ephelis, and Ema saw him calculate the moment of his brother's death against the timetable of what he considered an insignificant case.

His voice became hoarse with emotion. "Ema, did they kill my brother because they mistook him for me?"

"Perhaps, did you both still look very much alike?"

"Yes, even in later years, we could easily be mistaken for the same man."

"How many people knew you had a twin brother?"

"Hardly anyone, it was not common knowledge."

"Assassins are brought in from other towns for a good reason. Perhaps all they used was a picture of you in the newspaper."

"Yes, in those years they asked me to represent the department when providing public statements to the press."

Silence stretched between them again. Ep finally said, "There were never any other attempts against my life. Whoever wanted me dead could see I was still alive."

"Perhaps someone planned to kill your brother all along. However another party murdered him prematurely, thinking it was you."

"What are you saying? That someone else wanted to kill my brother?"

"You told me your brother's death ended your investigation."

"Yes, the news drove everything else from my mind."

"Perhaps the intent of murdering you, or in this case someone they mistook for you, was to end the inquiries into the disappearance of Annabelle Smith."

Ep stood up and paced back and forth, as he disentangled this logic.

"I think they made no further attempts against you because whoever ordered it, realized there was a much more powerful figure in the background that benefitted from their mistake."

"The only person who had reason at that time to want me dead was Levan Jackson, if indeed he was responsible for Miss Smith's disappearance."

"He understood very well how dangerous it is to go up against the most powerful men in the nation's capitol."

"Which are politicians," Ep finished her sentence.

THE DEAD CAST NO SHADOW

Ema reminded him, "You told me you were in ignorance of who would want to shoot your brother, or even why? That was before our visit with Joanne Goode. Ask yourself the same question now."

"There's only one person who fits the bill. Senator Gordon, whose daughter my brother abandoned to run off with a servant."

"What kind of man was he?"

"Well liked and voted in for many years by his constituents, however those behind the scenes knew he was as cutthroat as they come. He was not a man to be crossed."

"Perhaps Edward came to see you, but paid his father-in-law a visit first," Ema suggested.

"There's a good chance he did, but Ema as furious as Gordon could be over my brother's actions, which any father would be, doesn't mean he would pay for someone to murder him."

"Do you think Senator Gordon knew your relation to his son-in-law?"

"Most probably."

"Did he come to see you and report that his son-in-law suddenly disappeared? As his brother, you would be interested and offer assistance to find him. After the discovery of your brother's body, he could have spoken to you then."

"No, he never came to me." Ep said.

"Joanne said that your own brother described where Gordon would stop at nothing from protecting his family's reputation from scandal. Your brother's actions threatened to air out their dirty laundry again, rehashing his daughter's first divorce."

Ep turned to Ema with eyes that shone with fury and impotence. "Ema, as you've explained it, there were different reasons for targeting Edward and me for death. First, they killed my brother, and his death accomplished the result of why Levan Jackson wanted me dead. That's the only reason I'm still alive."

79

"Yes," Ema said, "or another possibility is that your brother was indeed just a victim of a random crime, but even if we are wrong about everything we've spoken about, one thing is clear now. Your brother fears for his daughter. He cannot protect her and wants you to do it for him."

The Art of Misdirection

The people in the lobby stared aghast at the woman walking in a wide-legged pantsuit next to the tall, white-haired man. In the last ten years, the populace came to terms with bobbed hair, dropped-waist dresses for women, with nary but a thin cotton slip underneath, but pants were scandalous and much too man-like.

Society matrons dipped their heads towards each other to air their grievances and outrage, now surer than ever the red-haired woman belonged to an upper-crust family that guaranteed her forgiveness, even after she flaunted the unwritten rules of ladylike decorum.

In response, Ep grinned and tipped his hat to them.

Ema saw the manager at the front desk direct a telegram messenger boy towards Ep, who gave him a coin for the cable.

He scanned it, and turned to Ema. "Gordon is still alive, but on his deathbed."

"What were you hoping for Ephelis, an eleventh-hour confession?"

"On the contrary, only reassurance he had nothing to do with my brother's death, and that Ed was plain unlucky."

"Why would you want to place that burden on your soul? I believe your brother would have met his end, if not that day soon after."

* * *

Ep and Ema crossed the street, and he opened his truck's door for her when a Ford with the police department's insignia drove up next to them; Sergeant Getty sat behind the wheel.

"Ep would you mind coming with me? I could use your advice on something."

"Sure, but she's not staying behind."

Getty misunderstood his intent and thought Lentigo wanted his secretary to take notes of any interesting story he could include in his memoirs. "She might not like what I've got to show you."

"She can handle herself."

Getty nodded, and Ed opened the backdoor of the car for Ema, and he joined the sergeant in the front.

A shoeshine boy outside the hotel's main entrance watched the car drive off. His task was watching out for police activity, and soon he'd meet with Mickey Pinto and pass on this information.

"So what's this all about Getty?" Ep asked.

"Lieutenant, I've got my hands full. Capone's living out on Palm Island, and our community leaders are not comfortable with public enemy number one, being a bit too indiscreet about his business ventures if you know what I mean. I've got President Hoover due to arrive in town in two weeks."

Ep nodded and let him continue.

"Last night someone robbed a huge shipment of sugar, which I bet is on a truck heading out west to the moonshine stills in the Everglades. I can take all that in stride, but there're some things I've never come across, and I'd appreciate someone like yourself with your experience helping with advice, that and the fact you'll keep quiet about this."

"I'll help if I can."

They drove towards the outskirts of the business district and parked outside the rubble-strewn entrance to an abandoned factory. A lone policeman stood guard outside the large doors, and he nodded as the group entered inside the dim interior.

Getty turned towards Ema, and cautioned, "This is not fit for a woman's eyes. Why don't you wait outside with my officer?"

THE DEAD CAST NO SHADOW

Ema gazed at him and replied, "If I get upset by what I see, I'll only have myself to blame."

Getty grunted and led them further in until they came to something suspended from a chain tied to a low beam on the ceiling.

The flayed body of a man hung upside down. Done so precisely his innards still sat inside the body cavity. Only the eye sockets were empty. The maroon figure with its arteries and defined muscles swayed slowly back and forth.

Ep and Ema stared at each other for a moment in complicit understanding.

Getty looked at the red-haired woman, waiting for her to faint or vomit, but she did neither. "She's a cool one," he thought.

He turned to Ep and said, "Lieutenant, I've seen plenty of dead men in my time, and God knows many of them died unpleasant deaths, but never anything like this."

"Do you have a name yet?" Ep asked.

Getty answered, "I'm not sure, but we found a taxicab crashed into a curb close to here, with no sign of the driver except for a shredded, bloody uniform."

The sergeant walked around the perimeter of where the body hung as he spoke, "The swamps west of here are littered with bodies, and that's why they're there, so nobody would find them. Most of them died with a bullet in them or benefit of a knife. Every once in a while we find a floater in the bay, but who in the name of God would do this to a man?"

"Someone with a very sharp knife and steady hands," Ep suggested. He sighed and continued, "Getty, I ain't sorry to say I've never come across anything like this. I'd say you need to confirm if it's the driver of that taxi and find out what he's mixed up in."

"I'm already working on that, but I feel like there's something…," he stopped at a loss for words, "something…"

"Evil?" Ema said.

Getty turned to her in surprise. "Yes, and I'm not a superstitious man, but I swear this is the handiwork of the devil."

Ep swallowed hard, thinking of how close to the truth Getty's suspicions were.

"What else have you found?"

"Nothing, nothing at all. No footprints, no signs of a fight, there's little or no blood around the body."

Ep thought to himself, "How do I explain this man's likeness was used to disguise a demon that attacked me a few hours ago?"

"Last thing I need is a maniac skinning people. Who wants to vacation in a town that harbors a monster like that? I guarantee Hoover, who's in Havana now, will bypass Miami and go someplace else until his inauguration if his advisers get wind of this."

From out front the officer called out Getty's name. They trudged back to the entrance, and the policeman whispered something to the sergeant.

"I'll be a son-of-a-bitch!" Getty exclaimed.

"What is it?" Ep asked.

"Taxicab company said the car was being driven by Malcolm Wagner, whose actual name is Malcolm Waxman."

"I take it Mr. Waxman is known to you already?"

"Yes, he got paroled from the State Prison Farm in Union County a couple of years ago. He was serving time for rape and the murder of his step-daughter. I ran him out of town, but life in the Glades is raw and hard. I shouldn't be surprised he drifted back in here, it outweighed his fear of getting pinched."

"Vengeance killing?" Ep asked, knowing full well that wasn't the case.

"Perhaps, but he served fifteen years of his sentence, and last I heard his wife died, and that's how he got paroled. There was no family to come before the board and oppose his release."

"Getty, why'd you really bring me here?"

"Lieutenant Lentigo, the first part is true, but you still got ties to the department in Washington. I'd appreciate it if you let me know if you receive word that Hoover has found out about this, and will avoid Miami."

Ep nodded his head. "I can do that."

"Well I guess I better take you back, and get the coroner out here."

They rode in silence, and Ema didn't speak until they sat in Ep's truck.

"Why do you think the mimic demon chose that man?"

"Because of his crimes?"

"In a manner of speaking; he put out an invitation many years ago. Like all open-ended invitations, you never know who'll take you up on it and when."

At Twilight Time

Joanne changed out of her uniform. Rachel who worked as a cashier at the corner drugstore wouldn't be home for another hour. Twilight shadows were falling across her yard as she sprinkled water on a small island of rose bushes in the middle of the front lawn.

Movement from the house across the street drew her eyes. A woman stood watching her. Even though daylight was fading, she made out her form. It took her a moment to realize the female figure appeared to be wearing a winding sheet. A sudden gust of wind blew her long black hair across her narrow shoulders.

"Hello?" Joanne called, knowing the property stood abandoned for over a year. The woman stood silent and did not reply. Something didn't feel right, and she shivered in the lengthening shadows.

"Do you live around here? Is something wrong?"

She jumped when the figure waved her hand as if motioning for Joanne to come closer.

Two streets over a shabby, sad motel occasionally discharged undesirables who meandered down this way, but it was rarely a woman.

She bit her lip, shaking her head in response to the bid to come to her.

A mad cackle burst forth from the figure shattering the unearthly stillness, and Joanne cringed as terror curved around her spine then rippled upwards.

Her instincts warned her that if she left the perimeter of the low, limestone fence around her property she would be at its mercy, whatever it was.

THE DEAD CAST NO SHADOW

She thought of Rachel, who meandered down the block after leaving her job, stopping to speak to neighbors who sat on their front porch enjoying the last hour of daylight.

She tried to reason with herself that perhaps this was a woman, who became disoriented or imbibed too much alcohol. After working in the hotel so many years, she witnessed many women acting erratically for several reasons, and sometimes they were more violent than men.

The figure again motioned, and something inside her shuddered in fear. A dark, siren call kept her feet pinned to the spot, even though a part of her struggled to gain release and protect her child. She sensed imminent danger lurked only a few feet away.

Steady headlights turned the corner down the street, and the spell broke. She realized she had been holding her breath. A vehicle stopped, and she saw a figure step from it and walk towards her. The figure coalesced and the feminine outline became sharper.

The breeze picked up and changed direction, bringing the scent of ripe putrefaction with it. Joanne brought an embroidered apron tied around her waist up to her face and covered her mouth and nose.

A sound like a child's rattle sounded out, no not a child's rattle but a snake's. The warning sound it gave when it sensed an intruder. Her eyes swiveled back to the figure where the noise originated from; the one who only moments before beckoned to her.

Like a person hypnotized, Joanne returned her gaze to the approaching silhouette and realized it was Ema, the woman who sat in her living room the day before. Something she held in her hand glowed and pulsed with a neon, turquoise light.

An arc of blue traveled through the settling night accompanied by the crack of a whip, and a feral scream followed it.

When she turned again to the property across from hers, she kept her feet under her by dint of sheer will. Where once stood a woman, there swayed back and forth what appeared to be a human-sized snake that ended in a woman's torso. At least four appendages, two on each side tipped with multiple, talon fingers moved back and forth.

Another crack of the whip echoed eerily, and the monster with lightening speed dove under the house. It scrabbled hard as it crawled fiercely into the narrow space.

Inside the truck, Ep hung onto his niece who fought to leave and run to her mother. Ema warned him earlier to intercept Rachel when she left her job, and they offered her a ride she readily accepted. He didn't understand why Ema told him to stop, but he did. With disbelieving eyes, Rachel and he saw the swaying, nightmare figure who confronted Ema, before it disappeared into the deserted property.

Ema wanted to pursue it, but with a creature so dangerous she could not risk the safety of Ep, Rachel or Joanne. It would strike out at one of them if she cornered it. And there was another problem; the stench that floated from the deserted bungalow was unmistakably that of a decaying body. They would have no choice but to notify the police.

She signaled to Ep, and he drove up. Rachel jumped out and ran to her mother, who stood in shocked immobility. He walked them inside the house, and came back to where Ema waited on the sidewalk watching the silhouette of the house, now cloaked in the darkness of night.

"I recognize that smell," he said tersely.

Ema turned to him, "When the police arrive, say nothing of what you saw Ep. Speak to Joanne and Rachel and explain to them you'll handle everything with the law, but they cannot say anything either. I suggest Sergeant Getty is the one who should come out here."

Ep nodded in agreement, and asked, "Will you be safe?"

"Yes, I will keep watch while you're gone."

Ema reviewed everything that happened since they crossed paths. She suspected that the Lentigo bloodline was the target. Did it begin when they were boys? But the family left El Paso and nothing happened to them except the fact that once you were marked as a member of the Dispossessed, you were one for life. She suspected a window of time would close soon, and the Lentigos would be permanently beyond the reach of the Evil that touched their lives many years ago.

Before long, Sergeant Getty stepped out of a police car driven by another officer. He came to where Ep and Ema waited for him.

Once he got a noseful, he shook his head and sighed. "Lieutenant, I see why you called me."

"My niece and her mother live in this house," he signaled behind him, "and they are both gone during the day at their jobs. Once they arrived, this abominable smell greeted them. They told me the property has been empty for over a year."

"Wouldn't be the first time a squatter dies in a deserted home."

"I thought as much, but you understand why I don't want to disturb these ladies. They are frightened as it is, when I suggested there might be a dead body there."

"I don't blame you."

He signaled to the waiting officer, who came with a flashlight, and they both crossed the street. Each headed in a separate direction around the exterior.

Ema told Ep the creature they saw fled off the property and the officers were not in any danger.

The younger policeman found a way in, and he exited through the front door where he came face to face with Getty. They both entered the house, and before long they returned.

"Whatever is causing the stink is under the house," Getty told Ep. "I'll have officers out here at first light to find whatever, or whoever is there."

"I appreciate that, please come and communicate with me directly, because I don't want to distress them any further."

Getty nodded his agreement, "I know where to find you."

Once he'd left, Ep turned to Ema. "I've convinced Joanne and Rachel to stay at the hotel. They are both so frightened they dare not stay in their house."

Once mother and daughter sat in the truck, Ema re-entered the home and created a glamour where their scent stayed strong in the home as if they were still occupying the structure. The creature bounded by its attraction to the occupants of the house would return, and this trick would keep it in the vicinity hoping to ambush them outside the circle of protection she laid down for them.

Upon their return to the hotel, they found another room became available on the same floor as theirs. Ep told them he would take each of them to and from their jobs until the police completed their investigation. He ordered room service for them, and a meal for Ema and him.

Suspecting that his brother might have visited his father-in-law in those days before his death, Ep called several sources which circulated among the Senator's staff or peers. However twenty years was a long time, and many were dead or no longer lived in the city. Reluctantly he called his son, Patrick an attorney who practiced law in Washington, D.C. and asked for his help as a last resort.

It therefore surprised him when a knock at the door was a messenger from the front desk. The young man handed him a sealed envelope, "Sir, you didn't stop to pick up your messages, and this arrived an hour ago for you."

"It's from Patrick," he said to Ema, as he scanned the paper. "I'll be damned," he exclaimed.

Ema watched him in silence.

"He found Gordon's secretary," He read the short telegram, "'The senator received word of his daughter's demise. No notice issued to the newspapers or peers about a death in the family. She remembers a man fitting Edward's description visiting Gordon a few days before'."

He tapped the paper against his finger, his thoughts fitting this last piece of information into the scheme of his brother's last hours. He said, "Well if there's ever a motive for murder, it's sorrow; especially if you blame someone for your daughter's death. I wonder what happened to her?"

Ep turned to Ema and stopped speaking when he saw the look on her face.

"What's wrong?" He asked in alarm.

"Joanne and Rachel are in great danger, more than I thought."

"How can I protect them?"

"They cannot return to the house, and you must get them out of the city immediately; the further and quicker the better."

Miami in the Rearview

Ema stood still by the curtain fluttering through the open window of her room. In the hush of the late hour, her eyes followed the shadows whipping in and out of the pockets of darkness cast by the construction equipment left in place by the crew working on the project across the avenue from where the hotel stood.

A human-like shape defined them; however they ran on all fours. Her presence would keep them well away, but these creatures were the retinue that accompanied a greater evil.

She could not be in two places at once, but Brother Miel and Mort wanted her to guard Ep, so despite her fears for Joanne and Rachel she would not leave his side.

Tomorrow she would tell him the only resolution to what hunted them would be to confront it in El Paso. He dreaded that prospect but it was unavoidable.

Then she admitted to herself, that helping the retired policeman reminded her of the many times she defied evil with Mort Peccatum her trusted avatar by her side. Since his death she had not replaced him with anyone. She purposely picked only pockets with the minimum animus to keep the body alive.

In the ten intervening years she hunted the most dangerous creatures and demons this side of hell. The fury with which she pursued them cut a wide swath among their number, but she admitted her intense dedication only distracted from the sorrow filling her heart.

In these last few days, she felt a surcease of the sadness that accompanied her everywhere. It was a bittersweet feeling; refreshing those memories she'd tried to bury. Loneliness was a high price to pay to deaden the longing to hunt with Mort by her side. It was good to help this family, but she held no illusion they were all in grave danger.

* * *

They were sitting down to eat breakfast, when a knock sounded at Ep's door. He'd already taken Joanne and Rachel to their jobs. Sergeant Getty stood there with a grim look on his face. Without being told they knew the reason for his visit.

Ep asked, "Who did you find?"

"We think it's a bum named Cheney."

"You're not sure?"

Getty's eyes flicked at Ema who sat sipping coffee. "There's not much left of him."

"What do you mean, and how did he end up under the house?"

"Ma'am," he spoke directly to Ema, "why don't you let me speak alone to Lieutenant Lentigo?"

"Don't worry about me," she responded, "just pretend I'm not here."

He turned to Ep and said, "I don't think he's been dead long, but it appears something ate him."

Silence stretched out between them. It was obvious the policeman expected ridicule. When he saw that neither Ep nor Ema responded in this manner, he continued, "Something hollowed him out. What's left is his head, extremities and spine, and there's no animal that'll do that to a human body. Something dragged and buried him in a shallow space, and I think he was still alive when it took him there."

"That's a very disturbing story," Ep commented.

"And before you ask, no he didn't have any enemies. He's known around town for doing odd jobs and drinks himself to sleep in many of the deserted houses in the neighborhood. He's a harmless old coot. I'm not sure how the coroner will rule on his death, but I thought you'd want to know what we found considering your family lives close by."

"Is this a warning?"

"Lieutenant, if I were you, I'd move them out of there; in case whatever did this comes back."

"I might just do that, maybe for a time."

"Lieutenant I know you're here in a non-official capacity, but I'd appreciate it if you accompanied me to the scene. Like the other murder we're trying hard to keep it out of the press, and I believe they'll do the same here and pass it off as the death of a homeless man. At this point I'll let my superiors try to figure this out, because I won't lie to you, I'm at a loss to explain how this man died. But I gotta look like I'm trying to find who did this, and I can use your help to satisfy them."

Ema whispered, "Ep, why don't you accompany Sergeant Getty? I can use your truck to pick up Joanne and Rachel. I'm sure they need to retrieve some personal items from their home, and we can meet back here."

For once the police officer smiled at Ema gratefully.

Ep asked him to recommend someone to shutter the house and maintain the grounds. Getty gave names of trusted men who would be glad of the work.

As they were about to leave, Ema spoke directly to Getty, "Sergeant I hope you take the advice I am about to offer, and do not dismiss it because you think I'm not a policeman, or worse a hysterical woman."

The meaning of her words was not lost on Getty, but he politely replied, "No ma'am, on the contrary I'll take everything you say to heart."

"For the next week, don't let your officers patrol that city block on foot, or worse by themselves once darkness falls. If they can, urge the neighbors to stay indoors at night. If one of your men must go out there for any reason, they should do it in pairs."

Getty's face blanched, and he looked from Ema to Ep.

"Listen to her, Getty. She's giving you very prudent advice."

He turned back to Ema and studied her with a speculative gleam in his eyes. He realized he'd made a mistake in dismissing her just as an assistant to Lentigo or a pretty bedmate. There was much more to her than met the eye.

"I'll take it under consideration because I can see the wisdom in what you're saying."

Ep took his hat and left the keys on the table. She carried out the plans they'd agreed to earlier. She packed their bags, went to Joanne's room and retrieved their belongings. Ema checked them out of the hotel, and waited by the truck while they loaded the luggage. Then she looked upwards and saw May's chalky-white face staring down at her from the fifth-floor window.

Her first stop was a nearby telegraph office where she sent off two messages. One instructed a deposit into a bank account in West Palm Beach, and the other was addressed to Mr. Harry Holbet who was wintering at the Breakers Hotel in the same city.

From there she drove to the Flamingo Hotel where Joanne worked. She was surprised to find Ema waiting for her in the lobby. She was even more shocked when Ema told her to notify her boss she was quitting. However, she remembered the tentative plans she'd made with Ep to leave the city, and go to his home in northern Virginia.

Once they were underway to pick up Rachel, Ema turned to her and explained that all she should retrieve from the house was personal items, a change of clothing and to leave everything else behind. Ema surprised her with an unexpected question. "Joanne, in those days you were with Edward in El Paso, was there anyone he mentioned that handled his affairs? A banker or an attorney?"

Ema studied the still pretty face of the blonde woman, who stayed quiet as she unfolded the pages of her memories. "Yes, there was a lawyer who came to see him once or twice that summer he was bedridden. I know he met with him once he'd left the house."

"Who was he?"

"A young man named Celestino Garcia. I asked him why he trusted such an unseasoned attorney, and he told me he had two reasons. One, he was intelligent and had integrity. Secondly, he was not in his father-in-law's back pocket."

By then they reached the small drugstore where Rachel worked. Within minutes they pulled up in front of Joanne's home, and both women entered the house. Ema waited across the street from where Ep and Getty stood watching as workmen excavated underneath the home in search of clues, or worse another body.

Ep excused himself and helped the women back into the vehicle. He purposely failed to tell Getty they were leaving the city within a few hours and their destination. He didn't envy the sergeant's predicament, but his family's safety was paramount now.

Once on the road, he turned to Ema, "Where to?"

"The Breakers Hotel, West Palm Beach," she responded.

* * *

It was a little after midnight, and Mickey Pinto sat in his car opposite the entrance to the Halcyon Hotel. Pierce had been dodging him for the last few days. He needed to a get a straight answer from him about who the tall, white-mustached man and the hot red-head accompanying him were. It was around this time the concierge left for home.

Personally he wanted to find out what happened to May and Georgina. Neither Cole nor he had any hand in ordering them smoked, so who did? Neither one of them bought the story that one dropped dead, and the other topped herself by stepping out the window of their room.

He lit another cigarette and let his gaze wander upwards towards the fifth floor, then he saw the flicker of a fluttering curtain and a white face filled by dark, unblinking eyes staring down at him. He stepped out of the car, unable to tear his eyes away because he recognized the curve of the face. It was May.

It was at this precise moment that Pierce pushed open the door of the hotel and came down the steps of the entrance. He stopped when he saw Mickey standing across the street.

Then a figure flew down like a weighted piece of white paper towards the sidewalk below. Both men saw a woman's body implode against the concrete without sound, inches from where Pierce stood. The rotund, little man gasped, fear not allowing him to draw a full breath. He fell over in a dead faint.

Mickey stood immobile, his mind trying to comprehend what he'd witnessed. The splayed figure moved slightly and stood up. May stared back at him with a crushed skull and rivulets of blood pouring down from her once beautiful face.

From that moment until he'd poured himself a second drink at the Frolic Cabaret with shaking hands did he realize where he was; everything else was a hazy blank.

Two days later he boarded a train Chicago-bound. He convinced Cole to give him half of the seed money they needed to start a small nightclub. They'd talked about it a million times, but stayed in Miami, hungry to rake in more cash by moving hooch around.

Months ahead of the Great Depression, he established a blues and jazz club he named May's Place, which survived despite the lean years of the 1930s.

Eventually Cole Deyo joined him there, but left Mickey to run the cabaret. During that decade of turmoil in Chicago spawned by gangster wars and union organizing activity, they found Cole shot dead in a back alleyway.

Mickey continued running the club. He never married and moved back to Miami Beach in the 1960s. He died in 1970 from heart failure. His friends remembered him as a nervous guy who told the best stories with a cigarette in hand. He had one idiosyncrasy though; he would never step inside a building with more than four floors.

The Edge of Darkness

Ema, Ep, Joanne and Rachel turned heads as they walked down the 200-foot long main lobby surmounted by a soaring vaulted ceiling. Sumptuous rugs, furniture and potted palms completed the richly appointed entrance to the Breakers Hotel, built by the railroad magnate Henry Flagler.

The manager at the front desk drew himself up with a disapproving mien and sniffed before asking what their business was.

Ema responded with a cool aloofness, "My name is Miss St. George, I believe Mr. Holbet has three rooms reserved for us."

Instantly the man's puffy chest deflated, and he quibbled nervously, "Yes, of course, Miss St. George, everything is in readiness." He signaled to a bell boy to come forward and directed him to pick up the luggage being held outside the front doors. They could not insult anyone connected with the influential Holbet and Van Alstyne families of New York under any circumstances.

As Ema requested the three rooms were interconnected. Since most of the day had been traveling, Joanne and Rachel rested in their room.

Ep sat down with a weary sigh in a well-appointed chair. He admitted that his bones ached. He was no longer the young man who rose at the crack of dawn and continued until midnight without feeling a twinge in his back.

"Ema, what happens next?"

"Tomorrow a local dress shop will come to our rooms, and I'll make sure Joanne and Rachel have clothing and coats appropriate to where they'll be living. A good friend of mine will secure a

99

private railway car to take them to Virginia. Let your son know to meet them."

Ep nodded. "And us?"

"We'll be heading to El Paso, it's the only way to stop what's stalking the Lentigos."

* * *

The next day a dressmaker came to the room and brought several unfinished outfits for the women. They took their measurements to tailor each one for them.

Ephelis rested and thought about what awaited him in the city of his birth.

A banker met with Ema in her room and brought her the amount of money she requested. He came from a little known bank that worked only with certain clients. Discretion and anonymity assured their existence in many guises for centuries.

Later in the afternoon, Harry Holbet came to the room and assured Ema he secured the transportation she requested in her message. Only his family knew of the history they shared with her and that despite the passage of time, she did not age. She appeared to be the same woman who smuggled his great-grandparents out of New Orleans in 1799. Their understanding was simple, provide her with help, no questions asked, and she in turn would act as a guardian towards their family as she had done over a hundred years before.

The day slipped away quickly, and the four dined together in their room. Ema thought it prudent to keep their presence out of sight of the public eye.

Once they finished, Ema went to the front desk and posted a letter to an address in Savannah, Georgia. This was the last place she held a permanent address, and the simple message explained she was staying in El Paso, Texas until her next notice.

The next morning the day dawned cool and cloudless, and the ride to the depot was short. Smoke coiled upward from the locomotive's stack as it prepared to pull out. The private railroad car set aside for Joanne and Rachel impressed Ep. He'd already sent word to his sons Patrick and Douglas who would take them to his home and settle them in. They agree to watch over the pair until he returned home. The thought came unbidden, "if he returned home."

Once they were underway, a middle-age man with silver, shoulder-length hair dressed in an impressive train conductor's uniform designed in a combination between a military officer and a chaplain entered the railway car. He introduced himself to Joanne and Rachel by stating he would look after all their needs during the trip.

Several days later, when they arrived at Ep's farm in Virginia, they would comment how much the groundskeeper who prepared the property for their arrival looked like this man, except the caretaker wore old overalls and a straw hat.

Ep in the meantime telegraphed his sons to let them know that he'd hired someone to open up the house and take care of the upkeep. The only information he gave about the man was that his first name was "Mike".

The Emissary

Ephelis and Ema headed northwest then west, planning to follow the Old Spanish Trail that would take them straight to El Paso. She told him it should take them over a week, and when he asked why so long, her answer surprised him.

"We only travel in the daytime; too many lonely stretches of road between here and there."

True to her word, an hour before sunset they found a small motel. Ema dispensed with the niceties of separate rooms. Two double beds would suffice. A greasy spoon down the street provided dinner and by 9 P.M. Ep snored softly, his troubles forgotten for the time being.

Hours later, Ema's eyes opened wide in the darkness. Ep's breathing still sounded regularly in the confines of the room. A sibilant noise brought her into sudden wakefulness. She recognized the sound of leathery wings rubbing against each other, large wings.

She did not become alarmed. The creature's intent was to track them, not to attack, at least for the time being.

The pair was ready to travel by first light, and the same pattern followed each day, where they found a place to sleep and eat by the time twilight fell. Ep communicated with his sons who confirmed that Joanne and Rachel reached their destination safely.

The last day before they arrived in El Paso, Ema directed Ep to a convent and school run by the Sisters of Mercy. He stayed waiting for her in the automobile, and when she returned, she directed him to park the truck inside a large barn that connected with a stone outbuilding that extended from the convent. Inside accommodations comprised two small cells with a bathroom. A young postulant brought them a simple meal later that evening.

Temperatures plunged once the sun set, and a fire crackled in a small fireplace of each cell. The midnight hour sounded from a bell tower in a chapel attached to the compound.

Ema disrobed and clapped her hands once and a swirling pool of Prussian blue opened under feet. It crept up her ankles and sheathed itself around her entire body. The skintight armor swirled randomly from darkest blue to purple as she moved. The only place not covered was her head and hands.

Her long hair braided itself. A small vase next to the bed held sprigs of bluebonnet that sprang to the air and twined itself through the burnished copper length.

She twirled her forefinger slightly. A ripple moved the air and opened up where a white glow pulsed from the aperture. She pulled her sword Zeruko Neskamea and the Iron Horse dagger into this dimension. Ema placed the long weapon against her back where her armor undulated and reached out to hold it like a sheath. The knife she placed into a special area in her abdomen which served the same purpose.

Somewhere in the convent, a group of nuns prayed the rosary. Chosen specifically because they were steadfast and strong in their faith, their voices murmured in unison.

Ema eased open a wooden shutter that covered the only window in the cell. Once outside, she stayed within the indigo shadows. A carpet of stars twinkled coldly in the heavens covered by clouds, and the short, high-pitched yips of coyotes in the distance broke the silence.

Ema sensed the energy of something that did not belong here; held at bay by a combination of prayer, holy relics and incense. A distant barn that once housed farm animals, but now disintegrated under the hand of wind, rain and sun drew her eyes.

She expected that what followed them through several states grew tired of watching. Sent as a spy, these creatures usually found this role difficult; their nature clamored to claim victims. Subservience was alien to them, even when threatened with punishment from a more powerful being.

It had not expected them to stop in a convent where the grounds were anathema to it. As sure as the day was long, now it plotted how to reach Ephelis before dawn broke over the horizon.

She closed her eyes, and like an animal sniffing for a particular scent she sent out feelers for the fuel that fed it. She sensed the source felt no remorse, loss or regret only an unending anger. And to think this was only an emissary and not the true enemy.

She opened her eyes and stared at the forgotten barn. From the far side of the gabled roof, an enormous hand grabbed the edge of a weathervane that still clung sturdily to the highest point. A powerful forearm pulled up a thickly built human figure eclipsed by wide, leather wings that flapped twice as it balanced itself. Even at a distance she made out the muscles that rippled under the mottled, lizard-like skin.

A hooked nose, pointy chin and protruding brow imitated a humanoid face, except the fangs and the spiked jaggy ears were found only in stone figures representative of gargoyles. A long, leathery tail whipped behind it as it stretched out its full length. Its hindquarters ended in feet tipped with curved talons.

Looking upon what trailed behind them, she realized it was not an assassin but a kidnapper. Its mission was to take Ephelis somewhere, and perhaps kill her if it could, but that was not its primary aim.

The ease with which it operated in this dimension divulged a very important secret. This creature had once been human, transformed into its present form either as punishment or reward, but making it unpredictable.

THE DEAD CAST NO SHADOW

Once again it stretched out its wings. It probably slept inside the crumbling structure. As if in confirmation, it yawned, exposing long canines on its upper and lower jaw.

Ema kept her cloak of immobility around her and narrowed her eyes as she studied the figure. Drawing on centuries of warfare with human and non-human enemies, she knew that if you can't breach a stronghold, then you make your opponent leave their refuge. The question was how this being would go about it.

The noise of the gate that led out of the inner courtyard squeaked in the nighttime silence. Keeping to the shadows she saw the face of the young postulant who served her food earlier, with a cloak over her shoulders. She paused at the expanse between the wall and the deserted barn.

There was only one reason a young woman steals out in the middle of the night to a crumbling outbuilding… the most powerful incentive of all, a lover.

She sighed certain that whoever waited for the young woman was now dead

The girl skirted the edge of the stone wall staying in pockets of murkiness until she had no choice but to walk out in the open. She was so preoccupied in staying hidden she failed to see the thing with gleaming eyes still perched on the roof of the barn that followed her progress.

Her cloak fluttering behind her, she hurriedly walked over to an old draw well with a wooden roof. The bucket suspended by a rope moved slightly from an itinerant breeze. She looked around to make sure no one saw her, then she sprinted to the far side of the tumbled down structure where the slats of a fence that once created a narrow paddock leaned haphazardly. She squeezed herself into an opening by where the wall rotted away.

When Ema looked upward, the space once occupied by the gargoyle was empty. She guessed it returned to the interior to wait for the girl.

Ema created a soft glamour which made her appear only as a movement that blended into her surroundings. She covered the distance in a thrice and followed quietly into the dimness where the postulant snuck in.

Once inside, the cold temperature caused her breath to fog. She looked down and narrowly missed tripping over the trembling body of the girl who scrunched into a fetal position. Her eyes were closed tight and Ema saw her lips move in silent prayer.

She looked up and saw the gargoyle reclined on a thick truss that stretched across the width of the sloping roof. Its thick hairless tail whipped back and forth like an impatient cat stalking its prey.

Ema crouched down, and with a sudden movement grabbed the young nun pinning her arms to her side. She covered her mouth with her hand and whispered into her ear, "Stay still and be quiet."

The girl jumped convulsively and nodded when she saw who it was. Ema smelled the sour scent of fear pour from her. And she looked up once more and saw the gargoyle raise its head and breathe in the odor. With a swift movement it bounded down to the rubble-strewn ground. It slinked towards where they lay hidden behind some crates.

"Do not leave here," Ema whispered.

Ema stood up, and the creature halted in its tracks. She strode purposefully forward, and with a hiss it backed away.

"Lady Sibyl," the gargoyle growled, "I have done nothing against you."

"Why are you here?"

"The scent of a sinner has drawn me close, and there is nothing sweeter than the virtuous betraying their vows."

THE DEAD CAST NO SHADOW

"Try harder than that. A young girl in love, no matter how virtuous or how sinful is worthy of your attention, or whoever sent you."

It stretched its frame upwards, measuring well over nine feet tall, and flapped its wings with a sharp snap to show its frustration.

It growled again, unused to conversation, but it dared not openly attack the Sibyl because then she would be within her rights to annihilate him on the spot. Annihilation meant being sent to a place of eternal light, truth and worse of all love, forever.

The young nun named Jacinta, opened her eyes and heard the woman speak an unknown language to the creature which responded in a guttural growl. All she thought of was to escape back to the convent. She stretched out her legs, and her sandaled feet met with something wet which rolled away from her.

She looked down in the oblique darkness. Now that her vision grew accustomed to the subdued lighting she searched for what lay at her feet. Two eyes stared back at her. It took her a moment to recognize the unblinking orbs. They belonged to Ciro the young man she came to meet. Terror flooded her being, locking a scream in her throat.

She closed her eyes, and when she opened them instead of Ciro, she saw a tabby cat that wandered about the kitchen feeding from scraps and the mice that inevitably crept about. It didn't move just stared back at her. She reached out to touch it, and from this new perspective it changed. The animal now resembled a dog crouching down with its head only inches from the ground. With an unblinking glare it faced her, and she realized its eyes were human. They were still Ciro's eyes.

Jacinta backed out through the opening, hearing a snarl reverberate from behind her. She straightened out, keeping the decayed wall against her spine. Her heart thumped hard against her ribcage. A throng of hyena-shaped, yipping shadows cavorted

107

in the space between her and the convent. Standing amongst them a jet-black humanoid figure with flaming eyes centered its attention on her.

Unable to contain her outcry, she shrieked at the top of her lungs.

Ema froze and saw the semblance of what passed as a smile curl the gargoyle's lips up.

She crashed through the rotted clapboard and came up next to Jacinta who wailed again in panic. Murmurs came from beyond the portico door leading into the nunnery.

The girl trembled and ran to stand behind Ema. The figure with the glowing eyes squatted down and an unearthly howl came from it. The shadows bounding around it stopped and yowled in imitation, sounding like a thousand lost souls.

Ema's eyes shifted to a figure that came through the partially opened entrance. It was Ephelis holding a pistol; she saw the frightened faces of several nuns behind him.

"Get them back inside and stay there!" She shouted at him.

He nodded once and pushed the women back, closing the heavy gates.

"It's him, it's him." Jacinta kept repeating.

"Who?" Ema asked, not taking her eyes off the figure.

"Ciro," the girl's shuddered, "he asked me to meet him tonight. He said I was so pretty, too pretty to lock myself away."

"So this is the sinner the gargoyle referred to," Ema thought, "little wonder he transformed into something ungodly once he'd finished with him. He wouldn't be the first one who sought gratification from corrupting the virginal."

The gargoyle hoped Ephelis would charge from the safety behind the convent walls to help Jacinta, however she was counting on his experience as a policeman to understand this was its aim. Right now she needed to get a hysterical girl to safety.

108

THE DEAD CAST NO SHADOW

A half moon hidden until then by the thick cloud cover illuminated the landscape in a metallic silver contrast as gusts of wind swept through the skies.

Ema swept her hand, palm forward counter-clockwise and plunged her fingers into a pocket that swallowed them, and she pulled out a pulsing, blue rod.

The crouching figure again raised its head and screamed, and the hunch-backed, four-legged pack around him joined in with a cacophony of anguish.

The blue rod she held, transformed itself into a whip she snapped, and it crackled with electricity that left a trail of blue static behind it.

"Silence!" Her voice rang out in an unnatural tone that caused the bell in the tower to clang out, and several items in the area rattled as if a tremor passed through the ground.

All sounds ceased, and behind her the gargoyle moaned in pain. The shadowy throng who did not have physical substance, ran in to murky crevices along the walls when the red-eyed shape snapped its teeth, and shook its head.

Jacinta in response ran up behind Ema and wrapped her arms around her waist, sobbing softly, and praying at the same time. Her thin frame shook with terror. Ema used the opportunity to move them closer towards the convent's entrance.

Then before her eyes the creature transformed himself into his last human incarnation; a handsome young man, with a thick mustache and a roguish smile.

"Jacinta, amor, what is wrong? Do you think I would hurt you?" His voice was normal and soothing.

She peered over Ema's shoulder at the man she had snuck out to meet. His uncle was a handyman who worked around the grounds, and he would deliver materials. He'd flirted with her for several months, finally convincing her to meet him in the ruined barn. His

109

compliments and the giddiness he caused her to feel, drove the first doubts about her calling as a nun. Lately she daydreamed of being married to him.

Ema murmured to her, "The man you met no longer exists Jacinta, do you understand?

The girl nodded vigorously against Ema.

"Trust me and understand that we must fight deceivers with their own weapons."

She nodded, and Ema squeezed her hands gripping her midsection. She raised her voice and responded in place of the young nun.

"Jacinta is now mine, and you will have nothing further to do with her. You are not worthy of her attention. She is promised to a higher cause. Get out of the way."

The dark-haired young man switched his attention to Ema. The smile faded from his face. An elongated, black tongue slipped out and caressed his lips before slipping back into his mouth. He replied, "Jacinta belongs to me, and I will have her one way or another. Even if I have to kill you and crush your bones before I sip your blood. Who do you think you are?"

Ema laughed out loud, "Who cares who I am, but I know what you are. A boy, just a boy pretending to be a man who cannot even conquer a full grown woman, and instead seeks a kind word from an inexperienced girl. I am sure genuine men spit on you, and will not allow you to be in their presence. They have no stomach for a groveling coward."

The creature, once named Ciro had not cast off the tether of his human personality. Fury transformed his features to what they had been moments before.

He growled, and from behind them, the gargoyle slapped its wings and flew down to where his new protégé stood.

"You foolish turd be quiet!" It commanded.

THE DEAD CAST NO SHADOW

Ema looked behind him, and saw Ephelis following the exchange from a small, barred opening in the door. He was ready in case he needed to pull Jacinta inside if she made a run for it.

Ema laughed out loud pointing at the gargoyle, "Even he knows you are filth and she will never be yours. The only thing you deserve are second-hand slops." She'd already guessed where his insecurities lay.

"I will not only have her, I will have you as well!" The Ciro Creature roared at her.

"And how do you plan to accomplish that?" Ema murmured in a deceptively soft tone.

The gargoyle growled at his newly minted acolyte who did not understand who he faced.

Ema turned to the bat-winged creature, "You should have gelded him right away; he will be your undoing. Would you like me to do it for you?"

Ema's eyes flickered across the distance and met Ephelis'. Once he'd overcome the shock of seeing the beasts that faced her, he understood her predicament exactly. He quietly unlatched the lock. Most of the nuns kneeled behind him in prayer, the others overcome with fear fled into the chapel itself.

In a swift and practiced move she exchanged the whip for the Iron Horse dagger.

"Considering there's not much to work with, it should take no time at all."

Ciro's human-like qualities submerged; his canines elongated and his hair grew long and scraggly. His back hunched and the scent of death came from him. They had made him into a scavenger meant to serve demonic beings in this dimension.

She saw his muscles bunch together, and in that split second when he launched his body across the space between them, she grabbed Jacinta by the wrist and threw her across to slam into the wooden door. Luckily the girl's build was diminutive, and she barely weighed more than a hundred pounds. With that movement Ema also sidestepped the attack.

Behind her the gate scraped and the cries of alarm from the nuns assured her they pulled Jacinta inside.

The imps that accompanied Ciro emerged from the gloominess and cavorted around them once again. His screech sounded like a rusted saw blade. He hissed and swiped at Ema with long and dirty claws that extended from his fingers. She stepped out of his reach with a speed difficult to register.

"Third time's the charm," Ema smiled coquettishly at both monsters.

"No!" The gargoyle moaned in despair. The Sibyl gave his creation more than ample opportunity to withdraw from the field without threatening her. In fact, she'd even given him the chance to intervene by the words she chose and he'd failed to punish his minion.

Like all freshly hatched hellish beings, loyalty was a foreign concept to Ciro. He considered the gargoyle's hesitancy in attacking Ema as fear, which in his mind made him the superior one in their relationship.

He charged her, swiping a clawed hand against his winged creator who stepped forward to intervene. Saliva drooled from the corner of his mouth while his oversized and pointy teeth gnashed in fury. All he desired was filling his mouth with Ema's warm blood.

When his body thudded into her, she fell backwards gripping him around the neck to keep his snapping teeth from sinking into her throat.

He was furious, strong and foolishly unafraid, believing he was invincible. Ema reminded herself this was a dangerous combination, and you can't intimidate an opponent who has no idea of your reputation.

They rolled on the ground as she got her body out from under him, and once she was on top, she straddled him and punched him fiercely on the side of his face, while holding him down with her other hand.

She saw the flash of surprise across his features when the force of her blows rocked his head. Little did he know that hundreds of years before, her sentient pocket had been a gladiator that cheated death dozens of times while the crowds in the coliseum roared for blood. She learned much about fighting during those days.

She cuffed him savagely across both ears making his head snap sideways.

He tried to buck upwards and throw her body off, but all it got him was a fierce blow to his solar plexus. His body sagged, and she hit him once more.

The gargoyle stood aside like an undecided referee. Not willing to intervene and deal with her, but ready to take advantage of a situation where he could claim victory.

Ephelis observed the fighting, and it stunned him to see what Ema wore. His first instinct was to help her but he remembered her instructions, and admitted he did not know how to battle the towering, winged devil that watched. He felt helpless, but he could not make things worse by being killed or captured.

Ciro got a knee underneath Ema and push her off. She fell backwards, rolled and regained her footing. He charged her once again, and she jumped over him. In a swift movement she came up behind him and wrapped her arms around his neck, squeezing hard as he struggled against her. He could not pull off the woman that clung to him with a terrible strength, despite his best efforts to shake her off or pull her arm loose from around his throat. His movements slowed until they ceased and his body finally went limp.

The blue whip materialized and turned into a turquoise lasso that wrapped itself around the immobile figure.

Ema, turned to the gargoyle, her dirty face tracked with sweat. In response it growled, curling back its thick lips and displaying the four large, curved canine inside its mouth.

"Who sent you?" She asked.

"I answer to none."

Ema sighed loudly, "This will be a brief conversation then. It is your misfortune to seek rest outside a convent where I am staying, but I will give you the benefit of the doubt and believe you are only an emissary and not a kidnapper. Therefore I will give you a message to deliver and be happy this is all I am doing."

The gargoyle flapped its wings in contempt. In an unexpected blur of movement, Ema pulled her sword forward and with a leap cut both its wings off. The creature yowled in pain, and the cauterized stumps smoked. Zeruko Neskamea glowed red with heat and then returned to its normal color. Within seconds of falling to the ground the bat-like wings disintegrated into ashes.

The gargoyle backed away from her, knowing full well she'd been merciful.

"This is my message: the man you sought to take is under my protection. Attacking him is equivalent to attacking me, and I am fresh out of mercy. The last of it I used on your underling."

Ema turned to the shadowy, hunchbacked figures who'd crept into the dim crevices along the wall and corners. "Take him back," she instructed.

Silently they converged on the gargoyle, and he struggled but they overran him and dragged him to the well. They plunged downward holding him in the middle of their numbers. There was a growl that echoed and ended in silence.

THE DEAD CAST NO SHADOW

Ema turned and grabbed Ciro by the scruff of the neck and dragged him inside the decaying barn. His body lay limp like a rag doll. There she dropped him, still tied down.

Once Ema returned to the convent, Jacinta came running and hugged her. The other nuns crossed themselves and trudged off to their cells. Ephelis stood apart watching the exchange. Now he understood why Brother Miel and Mort asked him to seek her out. Without her protection, he doubted he could have come this far, and he hated to think what would have happened to Joanne and Rachel.

"What are you planning to do with him?" Ephelis nodded toward the abandoned barn where Ciro lay.

"Once dawn breaks, what he became tonight will disappear. He will be nothing more than a man. Then I will need your help with the police, for I am sure that he is in hiding from the law."

Ep nodded, guiding her by the elbow toward where there rooms were. "Tomorrow then, but now let us both rest. You have my thanks, because in reality you do not know me, but you have protected me at every step."

She stayed quiet for a moment, and blinked a few times, however he saw that her eyes welled with unshed tears. "Mort would never send someone to me unless they needed my help. He is the one I would never refuse."

Memories of El Paso

Ephelis stood outside speaking to the sheriff of the little town.
Ciro sat handcuffed in the backseat of his police car. Another officer
stood by watching him steadily.

As Ema predicted, wanted for several crimes, Ciro slipped out of
El Paso to avoid capture. He'd grown a mustache and came to
work for his uncle until the heat let up.

Sheriff Martin shook his head, and said, "I can't believe he's
been under our noses all this time. I thought he'd left Texas by
now. He's always been on the wrong side of the law, and his crimes
have grown more serious. He's been part of a gang that attempted
a bank robbery. They were all killed, except Ciro who escaped."

"He tried to seduce a young nun."

The sheriff rested his hand on his gun. "He's originally from our
town, and I dealt with him since he's a teenager. There's something
cold about him, and I knew then he'd be more dangerous as he
grew older."

"Glad to help."

The sheriff regarded him for moment, and then asked, "You said
your name is Lentigo?"

Ephelis nodded.

"Any relation to the Lentigos who own the mansion on the
outskirts of El Paso?"

"Yes, why?"

"Few people know it belongs to the family of Senator Gordon
who died yesterday."

Ep looked up in surprise, "He did?"

"Yep, that old bastard's been hanging on. He's outlived everyone, including his wife and kids. Rich as Croesus, but mighty unlucky when it came to family."

* * *

It was a cloudless day, with winds blowing across the arid landscape. Ephelis told Ema about his conversation with the sheriff as they headed towards El Paso.

He asked, "How did Ciro become human again?"

"He transformed only hours before, and he had killed no one. Only this allowed me to reverse the curse placed on him."

Ephelis stayed quiet as he drove the truck. His mind mulled over everything that happened the night before.

"It's not a coincidence that Senator Gordon died at the same moment you've arrived here," Ema stated.

"That thought crossed my mind."

She directed him to an address.

"Where is this?"

"The law office of Celestino Garcia; Joanne said he was the attorney your brother went to during the time he lived in El Paso."

"She told you this?" He asked in surprise.

"Yes, he sought him out because he was not in his father-in-law's 'back pocket' was how she put it."

Within minutes of asking to see Celestino, he came out of his office into the waiting area. He stopped in his tracks when he saw Ephelis, then motioned for them to follow him.

Once the door closed he turned to Ep, "Your brother was my first client after they admitted me to the bar."

The well-appointed office, filled with mahogany furniture and luxurious decorations showed he'd done well for himself in the intervening years.

"Mr. Garcia, I've learned recently about my brother's life out here in El Paso."

"Well, it's saves me the trouble of finding you."

"How's that?" Ephelis asked curiously.

"Because your brother left explicit instructions that could only be carried out once his father-in-law died."

He went to the outer office, and told his secretary to cancel the rest of his appointments for the day.

Once they sat before his desk, Ephelis introduced Ema as his assistant. He assured Celestino Garcia he could speak freely about any matters that came up.

Ephelis started the conversation by saying, "Mr. Garcia, I am ashamed to say I lost contact with my brother for many years, and only now am I learning many things of what was going on in his life."

Celestino Garcia stayed quiet a moment as if picking his words before he spoke, "Mr. Lentigo, I think towards the last few years of his life, your brother did this on purpose to protect you."

"Protect me? From what?"

"Once he learned how manipulative his father-in-law was, he feared this man would somehow embroil you in his political peccadillos, especially since you were a police officer in Washington, D.C."

"Somehow I know there is more to my brother's story than this."

"Yes, and even though I will have a formal reading of his will in a few days, there's no harm in telling you what I know about him."

Ep nodded his head in agreement.

"Your brother was quite a wealthy man."

"Wealthy?" Ep asked, "I know that he married Senator Gordon's daughter, but not much beyond that."

"You are right, however for many years he bought certain mines out in the Southwest. Initially, he thought they were duds, but

118

some turned out to be lucrative. However, after his marriage to Stella Lentigo he kept investing in buying others, but," and here he paused for emphasis, "he disguised ownership though business names which I helped him set up. He wanted to keep his involvement in the mines hidden."

Ephelis traded looks with Ema, wondering if this was the reason for his brother's murder.

Celestino Garcia continued, "However that is not where the true bulk of his wealth came from."

"From where then?" Ep asked.

"His wife Stella."

"Her, but I thought it had been a marriage of convenience only?"

"Yes it was, but in truth Stella was indifferent to your brother; however she hated her father; deeply hated him. So she made a will soon after her marriage that left her entire fortune to Edward Lentigo. By then she knew she could not have any children, but she wanted her father to know he, or none of her family would inherit any part of her wealth."

"I would have thought her money came through her father."

Celestino laughed mirthlessly, crossed his arms and continued his story, "No on the contrary, she was an heiress in her own right. Her mother, Senator Gordon's first wife, came from a prominent family in the area. Rumors were that is why Gordon married her to begin with. It was her money that propelled him into a successful political career, however it was understood that her fortune would always go to their children and not him should she die. That's exactly what happened, she died and their only child was Stella."

"So Stella became a poor, little rich girl?" Ep asked.

"I cannot think of a more appropriate description. The child was wealthy, but poor when it came to affection. Her father remarried soon after becoming a widower and had two other children. From what I understand he showered them with his approval, however

Stella was under the care of a governess and then off to boarding school."

Ep said, "I learned about the unfortunate circumstances of her marriage to her first husband and the scandal of divorce that followed."

"Poor Stella was star-crossed when it came to love. From what I understand, both her husband and the man she later ran off with both became involved with her because of her fortune," Celestino clarified.

He paused, and continued, "For many years nothing untoward happened. She ordered the Lentigo mansion built to her specification. She limited her social interactions only to the prominent families of the area. Your brother did as he pleased as long as he played the role of the dutiful husband and did not embarrass the Gordon name."

"And then my brother fell in love with the help," Ep stated matter-of-factly.

"Yes and no. I think Stella would have overlooked a dalliance, even a mistress kept out of the public eye, but not being abandoned for all to witness."

"I'm surprised she left everything to my brother, anyway."

"That was not her intention until fate intervened. Based on a recommendation from your brother, I infiltrated a couple of servants into the household that reported on the going-ons. The story I heard was that she had been out riding with a group of supposed friends, and one of them made a cruel remark that perhaps her husband ran off because he wanted to have a child. They described where she grew frenzied and said something about going to see her lawyers right away."

"And did she?" Ep asked.

"That afternoon the horse she rode threw her. Some said it was because of a snake. She lingered only a few days unconscious and without being able to change her will. I negotiated the disposition of her estate by proxy with her lawyers as your brother's representative, and he inherited all her fortune."

"Soon after, my brother was killed?"

"Yes, but Mr. Lentigo your brother was very astute. He'd always left his affairs with certain instructions to protect his estate whether he died or disappeared. Throughout the years the Lentigo mansion stood shuttered but maintained, as were all his properties using the funds set aside specifically for that purpose. His only caveat hinged on Senator Gordon's death, and his wife's as well."

"He didn't know about Mrs. Lentigo's death?"

"I don't believe so, because he died soon after she did."

"Mr. Garcia, I came here hoping to find answers to why someone killed my brother, but I have found only more questions. I'm surprised Senator Gordon did not challenge his daughter's will."

"I wondered about that, but she predeceased your brother, and he legally inherited all her wealth. The last thing he wanted was to drag his family through another scandal and damage his political career. I hope what I've told you helps but as a result you are a very wealthy man Mr. Lentigo."

"No, I'm not." Ephelis responded quietly.

"Yes you are, the condition stipulated by Edward has been met."

"My brother has a child."

"What?!" Celestino Garcia came to his feet. "A child?"

"Joanne Goode gave birth to a daughter named Rachel, I met them only a few days ago."

Celestino sat back down and drummed his fingers on his desk. "Are you sure this is Edward's child?"

"Her birth corresponds to approximately eight months after my brother's murder, and her appearance leaves no doubt she is my niece."

121

"Your brother includes mention of any children born to Joanne and him in the will. It was only normal that he considered they would be together and children would be born of their relationship. Where are they now?"

"In Miami, and I believe my brother left them there hoping to hide them in obscurity. Joanne proved to be a very resourceful woman, and she was able to bring up her child safely."

"Yes, I remember the day he came to visit me before leaving El Paso. I'd never seen your brother this worried. I wasn't sure if Senator Gordon was here or in Washington and perhaps they argued."

"Did he tell you what happened?"

"All he told me was that he'd met with Stella, and he left El Paso the following day."

Celestino told Ephelis he needed the rest of the day to prepare all the paperwork tied to the Lentigo estate, and to meet him the next morning at the mansion.

Ema and Ep headed towards a hotel recommended by Celestino.

She turned to him and commented in a dry tone, "I noticed you told Mr. Garcia that Joanne and Rachel were in Miami and not in your home in Virginia."

"My brother trusted him, but that was almost twenty years ago. Time changes people, and until I know differently, their whereabouts stays between us."

He suddenly turned down a side street that led towards the outskirts of El Paso.

To Conquer Evil

Off the northwest horizon a stiff wind blew down from the Franklin Mountains swirling dust and torn up debris against the scattered tombs poking up between clumps of salt cedar, cow-tongue cactus and lechuguilla. Some gravestones were wooden and plain, with names painted crudely on them; the graveyard itself seems overgrown and unmaintained. Ep stopped outside the gates of the Concordia Cemetery.

He turned to Ema and said, "This is where Eddie and I found the cavern. Somewhere out there; back then it wasn't officially a graveyard just part of a ranch and the San Jose Church and a few tombs around it."

"A cavern?" Ema asked.

"Now that I think about it, it was probably an old crypt, but for a couple of kids, we thought it was a cave because we saw some stone steps leading down. I remember that winter was real dry and when summer rolled in we had days of thunderstorms and rain. We were out of school, so when the weather cleared up we were itchin' to play."

Ep stopped speaking, his attention caught by a sudden movement between two obelisk memorials. Ema followed his gaze and saw the soft oval of a woman's face peering at them from behind one stone. She wore a high-collared white shirt that contrasted with the café au lait tint of her skin. Her dark hair piled high on top of her head in a swirled pompadour style favored by women over fifteen years before bespoke that she was not of this time.

Ephelis looked back at Ema and said, "She knows where we came from."

123

"She does?" Ema asked softly. "How do you know?"

"She said Florida."

"That's her name," Ema murmured.

"What?"

When they looked again, only a stretch of monuments and crosses faded off into the distance.

"Did you see how easily they speak to you Ephelis?"

"Yes, but I don't want to." He stated staunchly.

"I understand better than you think, but remember you are no longer a helpless child, but a full grown man who has faced many dangers in his life and triumphed over them."

"Why are you telling me this?"

"Because just like when you deal with the living, fear is used against you."

The dry desert wind picked up speed and howled as it swept across the terrain.

Ep took his hat off and combed back his tousled hair with his thick fingers. He sat back in the truck, leaned his head on his hands and looked up at Ema.

"Being out here reminds of when I was a kid. Eddie and I saw things no child should witness."

"What did you see?"

"The wind was blowing like today, except it was oven-hot. We went down these shallow steps, exploring like any red-blooded boys would. We were on an adventure, and at first we didn't realize that even though the path kept going down, there was always some source of light illuminating our way."

"It opened up into a chamber, because that's all I can call it. There was a tall girl standing there waiting for us. Long, wavy brown hair framed this beautiful face with wide blue eyes. And she spoke to us in this soft, light whisper, 'Boys, leave now.' There was this wonderful scent like spring rain coming from her."

124

"Did both of you see her?" Ema asked.

"Yes, and you would think we would have run away, but it felt like a dream. A hot wind boomed against the walls and she faded away. Everything around us shimmered and expanded. There was this figure dressed in a dark cloak, but the hood of his robe covered his face. He had all these silver bars arranged around him, and gold coins with other jewels that winked in the light. I remember Eddie looked at me, and I stared back and his eyes were as big as saucers. We were children, and I think this made it easier for us to accept without questioning how impossible it was."

"How did that figure make you feel?"

"Startled at first than it talked to us in this hoarse softness like a hiss; you couldn't tell if it was a man or a woman."

"What did it say?"

"All these riches would be ours, and we thought of making our family happy and wealthy. Our father worked hard at a small post office and grocery store in the middle of town. We barely scraped by."

"What did it want in exchange?"

Ephelis looked at Ema and stayed silent a moment. "How do you know it wanted something?"

"It always does."

"It said only one of us could have it. We would have to fight one another. The winner would keep the treasure and be able to leave."

"So this is the only thing it wanted in exchange?" Ema asked softly.

"We saw these terrible scenes in our minds. It wanted us each to fight the other, but to the death. This is when we became terrified. I remember Eddie took a stone and threw it at the figure, and that's when we saw what hid under the cowl. It was a lizard, but it looked like a man at the same time. Bright, yellow eyes stared at us. It was horrible! Even as children we understood we were in acute danger. We backed up, realizing it had no intention of letting us leave."

Ep's voice quavered as he recalled those moments. He continued, "It hissed as we inched towards the opening, afraid to turn our back on this thing. Suddenly we became aware of someone behind us, and I think we almost died of fright."

"When we turned there was a tall man there dressed like a conquistador. We'd seen pictures in lessons at school. He took us by the shoulder and pushed us out in front of him through the tunnel. He followed and we heard this thing hiss again, and other voices screamed and growled."

He continued, "Once we got outside, he said in this quiet voice something I never forgot, 'Never return, ever. And tell her I've repaid her for my freedom.' We ran out into the hotness of the afternoon. I looked over my shoulder and saw this man fade into the sunlight."

"What happened then?"

"We got home and went to our room. We said nothing to our mother, because she'd warned us not to go there. Strange things happened in our home, and the truth came out. Nightmares tormented us, and I compared notes with my brother. We were dreaming the same thing. Strange shadows would come into our bedroom at night, other times we would see horrendous faces looking in through the windows of our house. It got worse and worse. My parents called the parish priest, who did his best with blessings but it was plain that he could not stop what was happening."

"When did everything change?"

"It was November, a long four months, and one day the priest brought this tall, bearded friar he called Brother Miel. He asked us to tell him what happened, which we did. He stayed at our house, and that was the first time we could sleep through the night, and our house became peaceful again. During those days, he performed several blessings, and warned us never to return there. Later we learned that he told our parents to move us away from El Paso as soon as possible. Five years later we left for Chicago."

"Did you ever tell your parents about the girl that warned you away from there?"

"Yes, we did. My mother ran off crying to another room when we described her. My father told us we had an older sister that died about a year before we were born from scarlet fever. She would have been about the age we described if she'd lived. We never knew she existed."

Ep studied Ema for a moment, and continued in a quiet voice, "The conquistador's thanks were meant for you. Am I right?"

"Yes, you are. A very long time ago his soul was in the grip of great wickedness when I freed him."

Ema looked off into the distance; her cheekbones flushed pink from the cold bite of the breeze that flowed around them.

"There was something else Brother Miel told us, even though we were children. He said something like this if memory serves me, 'You are now members of the Dispossessed, as am I. You have beheld Evil, and you can either triumph over it or become its slave, but you can never outrun this. The Dead will try to converse with you because they will hope you can help them, or if they are dark, they will try to seduce you. You are both powerful because goodness dwells in your heart. For this reason Evil will try to corrupt you throughout your life, never allow it entry.' He left the next day, and we never saw him again."

"It appears you took Brother Miel's advice."

"I never wanted to reminisce about those days again even with Eddie. Before we were ready to leave for Chicago, he tells me he thinks he knows what that place was, and that's when I realized somehow it fascinated him. I argued with him I didn't want to hear

127

another word, but he convinced me. He described the Lost Padre Mine. The legend was that Jesuits left their treasure buried out there sometime around the 1500s. He didn't get any further before I punched him in the mouth. That was the last time he talked to me about it. I was sorry as all hell I hit him, but I was more scared than sorry."

The conversation ended, and they headed back towards the hotel. Again they booked adjoining rooms.

Colorful Navajo rugs covered the dark floors of the room. The bellboy dropped the luggage off and lit the fireplace before leaving. Overstuffed, brocaded furniture welcomed Ephelis and Ema, and she wasn't surprised when his head nodded forward as he napped. She left him a note to say she would be back soon.

Mistress of the House

Delphine Guerrier born a bastard, luckily claimed a wealthy man as her father. When the Civil War swept through New Orleans it reduced his circumstances, however he still kept enough funds to house his favorite mistress, Helene in a small, well-appointed townhouse. Jacques Guerrier had a legitimate family, however he truly loved Helene, and he was heartbroken when she died in childbirth in 1875. He placed their five-year-old daughter, Delphine with the Ursuline sisters at their convent in the Ninth Ward assuring she would be well-educated.

The sisters ran the Ursuline Academy, a boarding school for Catholic girls born into privileged circumstances, but there was always space for girls born on the wrong side of the blanket, especially when her *Péré* gave money to the sisters. She apprenticed to a nun who acted as a pharmacist for the convent. Young Delphine learned how to treat the sick and wounded who came to the Sisters' hospital.

Her world came to a heart wrenching end when her father died. She was fifteen years old, and she came under the protection of her older, half-brother Alexander who she had never met.

The mother superior called Delphine into her office one day, and even though her eyes were kindly, she was blunt and to the point.

"Delphine, I have met with your brother Alexander and he came to tell us he can no longer provide any money for your education. Based on our conversation, you can either become a postulant to the order, and I know you have no calling for this, or… " and here she paused choosing her words carefully and then continued," he can find you a husband. He mentioned a man's name which I know is married and has children your same age. Your brother believes that because we live inside convent walls we do not understand the outside world. In other words, your brother is selling you off to become a whore, not a wife. You have seven days to ponder and pray on your decision."

The mother superior opened a small box in front of her that held jewelry and some coins. She closed it and pushed it across her desk to Delphine. "This is a small dowry your father held for you along with your mother's jewels. It belongs to you now. Be prepared to give me an answer when I call for you again. You may go now."

Even before Delphine returned to her room she decided, and it was neither of the ones offered by Mother Superior. She would leave New Orleans and make her own fate, but her first problem was where to go. She was naïve about most things, but she was astute enough to recognize that if she stayed in the city, her brother would find her and deliver her into the hands of a stranger.

An answer to her prayers came three days later when Annie Hunter, a classmate disclosed to her to that she planned to run away back to El Paso, where her parents lived. Her father shipped her to the nuns with instructions to refine her manners and polish off her rough edges. He was a nouveau riche cattleman that hoped his daughter would return ready to rope in a wealthy husband. The problem was that Annie was desperately homesick, and she confided to Delphine that once she was there, he would not have the heart to send her back.

When Delphine volunteered to accompany her, Annie was ecstatic. Two years older than her friend, Annie secured passage on a train for both of them and masterminded their escape. On the seventh day when Mother Superior expected an answer from her, Delphine sat with her friend heading westward toward Texas and an unknown future.

However like all best laid plans, Fate intervened to remind them they were at her mercy. Annie waited until the last stop before reaching El Paso to telegraph her father when she would be arriving. To her surprise, the person who waited at the depot was not her father but a man named Jason Gallagher, a business associate that occasionally came to her parent's home. His solemn face raised an alarm in her heart. He refused to tell her why her father had not received her. When they reached Annie's home, the answer became obvious. Another man shot Mr. Hunter. Delphine later learned that it came about because of a lurid love triangle that played out in a brothel.

Annie's offer to have Delphine stay with her evaporated when she learned of her father's death, as her older brother embraced her when she stepped out of the carriage and told her the news. A family in mourning had no time for an orphaned runaway.

Jason offered to have Delphine stay with him, and in truth how could she turn him down. She had nowhere to go.

In short order Delphine came to understand the reality of her new existence. Jason one time gunslinger turned gentleman gambler, owned a prestigious saloon that sat cheek and jowl with an upscale brothel. Each business benefited one from the other; however they only received men with deep pockets who sought the company of lovely women, enjoyed high-stakes card games and the finest liquor.

Jason lived on the third floor of his saloon. That night he sat with a bottle of AA whiskey and listened to Delphine's story; like mother superior at the convent, he came quickly to the point.

He told her he would claim her as his mistress to safeguard her from the attention of other men; however it was not in his power to spare her reputation, which was shredded once she set foot through the door of his establishment.

Delphine's face became taut with caution, wondering if becoming his mistress would be the price of her safety.

Jason Gallagher laughed mirthlessly and assured her she had nothing to fear. After a gunfight a bullet wound that failed to heal properly left him impotent. He warned her that now she was the recipient of a well-guarded secret. If she ever disclosed it, she would find herself whoring in a one-room crib in the grimiest street of El Paso's tenderloin.

Delphine understood only too well that her safety depended on her ability to play the part of a pampered mistress. Later she was to learn that Jason's fierce reputation as a gunslinger and lawman guaranteed few men or women would voluntarily cross him.

In return for his altruism, Jason discovered that with her gentle touch and her knowledge of medicine and pharmaceuticals, Delphine chased away pain that hounded him for years, and made him appear older than his correct age.

As he predicted once she became a fixture in his apartment Annie discontinued their friendship.

A year later madams Alice Abbott and Etta Clark, once friends battled over a young prostitute named Bessie Colvin in the tenderloin of El Paso. Etta ended up shooting Alice who miraculously survived. On May 13, 1886 a jury found Etta not guilty on grounds of self-defense after they charged her with attempted first-degree murder.

The sordid but comedic gunfight between the brothel owners resulted in a surprise conversation between Jason and Delphine, or Dolly as they now knew her. Envious patrons of the saloon looked at her with hot and hungry eyes the few times she left the apartment.

Jason and Delphine became close and fell in love, but the reality of their present circumstances prevented a consummation of their feelings.

He told her he was dying. Jason pointed out that once she was alone, within hours of his demise a greedy madam would swoop in to claim her as a money-making prize, especially when they discovered she was still a virgin. All he asked was that she continue to trust him.

A few weeks later a tall, fair-haired man that Jason introduced as Mort Peccatum a good friend visited the upstairs apartment. Delphine hid her surprise, because Jason allowed no one entry to their private quarters. After an afternoon convincing her she had to leave before he died, she finally agreed when a physician that treated Jason confirmed that he had only weeks to live.

Mort escorted her to Savannah, Georgia where she met a woman named Ema, the owner of an apothecary shop. It was here she completed her education in using chemicals, herbs and medicines. She also confirmed the true nature of Evil and its existence in this world, something only hinted at in her teachings at the convent.

Five years later she returned to El Paso and established her own druggist shop using the money left to her by Jason Gallagher and supplied by Ema's apothecary in Savannah. She was young but intrepid and put into practice everything she learned as Ema's apprentice, and her business flourished.

Despite her belief that her heart would never heal from Jason's death, she fell in love with a wealthy miner. They married and had several children.

The afternoon she met with her mentor, the fifty-nine-year-old Dolly Andrews, as she was known then, was a respected doyenne of El Paso society. No one remembered that many years before she'd lived over a saloon with an infamous gambler.

Stella Lentigo

A servant closed the door of a parlor where Dolly and Ema enjoyed a cup of tea. Ema looked no older than when she first laid eyes on her in 1887. This did not surprise her. There were many things she learned as Ema's apprentice, and one of them was that what many in her world knew as reality was anything but that.

They spoke about their lives, the good, the bad; the mundane and the surreal. When Ema told her of Mort's death in 1919, Dolly in a whisper expressed her condolences because she knew by looking at her how affected Ema still felt about this loss.

Ema asked her, "What can you tell me about Stella Lentigo?"

Dolly gave a short laugh, "Well there's a name I haven't heard in quite some time."

"Perhaps when you returned to El Paso she had another name?"

"Back then we didn't move in the same circles, but she was the talk of the town. She scandalized everyone by cuckolding her husband and running off with one of his business partners. She'd been embarrassing her father though since she was just Stella Gordon, and he was sadly disappointed to find out that marriage had not brought her to her senses. It was only her ties to him that kept all doors from slamming in her face."

Dolly regarded Ema and continued, "Your interest in the late Mrs. Lentigo is anything but coincidental, and you really don't care if she offended the upstanding citizens of El Paso."

Ema smiled and nodded, reverting to her real name, "Delphine you are correct, outraged sensibilities are a fleeting thing."

"I will tell you what I know, and how much of this is truthful I'm not sure, but I think much of it is. Even before she ran off on her husband, there were whispers that he might seek a divorce

134

because after ten years of marriage there were no children. He knew it wasn't him because he had a child out of wedlock before standing at the altar with Stella. She was not so easily convinced, even back then she was as prideful as she was beautiful. However there are some truths you can't escape from and this was one of them. Her lover deserted her, and she'd given her husband ample excuse to seek a divorce based on her adultery."

"So all she got for her troubles was humiliation," Ema observed.

"Yes and it was a hard lesson learned, because after that fiasco she laid low, society-wise that is." Dolly said. "Fresh scandals drove her name from the front page of the newspaper and the years moved on. She quietly remarried and became Stella Lentigo, and I remember only a mention made of a large house built on the outskirts of town for the new couple. However," and here Dolly paused and smiled with a knowing look in her eyes at Ema, "mutterings never repeated in proper society swirled about her. They commented that her companions or friends if one could call them that, were a jaded and cruel lot. Talk of orgies, drug use and other distasteful practices followed her reputation like a swarm of flies. Her marriage was only a sham, concocted by her father to lessen the damage caused by his daughter's action."

Ema nodded, as if confirming something she already suspected.

"Her name once more appeared on the front page of the newspaper describing her death after being thrown from a horse. What they omitted was that her husband had run off with a young maid who'd taken care of him when he recovered from injuries only a short time before she died."

A silence pregnant with expectation stretched between them. Dolly said, "Ema, I imagine you already heard most of what I recounted, but you are here seeking darker waters than whatever tabloids printed about Stella Lentigo."

Ema smiled enigmatically at her and said, "Then tell me what you've heard through the years; perhaps stories that many discount as lies or superstition."

"Very well, most of it had to do with the Lentigo Mansion, because what else can be said about someone who's dead, except that they're haunting the place they used to live at."

"And was she?"

"Perhaps, but I'm not sure. An empty house even with manicured lawns still develops a reputation. Her family never visited, and her husband never returned. Some whispered that he'd died only a few days after her, and I think that's when whispers started about it being cursed. It's a large enough property that they installed a caretaker to live on the grounds, but they didn't stay long. Stories were told, mostly by servants that strange shadows lurked inside the house, and they saw grotesque figures lurching about in the gardens that surround it."

"What figures?" Ema asked.

"Animal-like, but not human either. There was no romantic lady-in-white, only something that profoundly frightened the staff so much they couldn't hire anyone to live there. Those who came to clean the interior did so for a few days every month, but left before the sun set and the same thing for the gardeners."

"What else?"

"Both her lover and her first husband died by their own hand. Shortly after the scandal, each moved to Austin. One practiced law and the other went into local government; they married, had children and prospered. Within a year of Stella's death, her first husband slit his throat with a razor and the lover hung himself inside the closet of his children's nursery. These were bizarre acts of self-destruction because there was no indication they would do this. They left no note behind either."

THE DEAD CAST NO SHADOW

It was at this precise moment that stillness filled the room. Even though daylight filtered through the partially open windows, shadows lengthened and stretched themselves from floor to the tall ceiling, turning the late afternoon into night.

Dolly's eyes widened and her gaze met Ema's in alarm, however she stayed silent. The stale odor of the grave long unopened surrounded them.

Ema's eyes followed the movement of a dark mass that exited through the opening of the unlit fireplace.

A low rough voice in a language only Ema understood came from it, "So you speak of my handiwork?"

"Did you know these men?" She asked.

"No, but their destruction gave me pleasure, nonetheless."

"Then you did it at the behest of another." Ema stated with certainty.

"What matters the reason, I have come with a warning."

"What do you want in exchange?" Ema asked.

The sound of a dry, mournful wind swirled through the room. A stealthy whisper tempered with an urgent rhythm answered, "Only your favor Red Lady, only your favor."

"As a being of misery, if you do not serve another, then you only serve yourself. Deliver your warning, and I will decide if there is any worth in it."

"Your absence is noted, and there are those who fear another more than you. They only wait for the sun to surrender to the night before they take the man you guard. Even now they gather hoping you will not be there to defend him."

In seconds the shadows retreated, and whatever used the opening of the chimney slithered backwards the way it arrived.

Ema's looked out through the window where the sky shimmered in different shades of blue, and already the sapphire brilliance of the afternoon disappeared towards the violet of nightfall.

Dolly looked at Ema, aware that something conversed with her in a manner she did not understand, but the taste of corruption lingered in the air and her human soul shrank from it.

Ema stood up and hurriedly put on her coat and hat. She asked, "Dolly do you remember how to put down a boundary of protection around your property?"

Without a moment's hesitation she answered, "Yes I do Ema; do not worry about me, I have forgotten nothing of what you taught me."

Ema flew out of the house, and the truck spit out gravel behind it as she gunned the motor and turned out of the driveway in front of the Victorian mansion, and onto the road.

She glanced westward, watching the sun dip towards the horizon, and she raced towards the hotel as the yellow spangles danced against the pinkish clouds hoping she could save Ephelis.

Absalom Sparks

Ema stopped the truck in a narrow passage behind the hotel.
As luck would have it, their rooms were on the first floor, and she
calculated which windows opened to their quarters. Bound by the
etiquette of the day, and in some places the law, they forced her to
have a separate room from Ephelis, and she opened the casement
left ajar to the one assigned to her.

Once inside she eased out of her coat, and then the sounds of
furtive movement came from the small closet behind her. She
inched towards the door and opened it slowly. She met the barrel
of Ephelis' Colt pistol pointed at her.

"Dammit, Ema!" he whispered in a mixture of exasperation and
relief.

"Is there more than one?" she asked quietly.

"I think so. I came in here looking for you when I smelled
something like rotting garbage coming from my room. That's not a
good thing, is it?"

Ema shook her head and told him quietly, "Stay close to me."

Ephelis nodded. He looked down and saw her pull out the
shimmering dagger that she'd used to kill the Mimic Demon.

The door between their rooms opened further and Ema saw
Ephelis' would-be kidnapper. An emaciated, gray-skinned,
cadaverous figure crept in. Naked except for a long, bedraggled
loincloth; tangled dirty hair draped over its back and chest. In place
of a human head, a horse's skull jutted forward with a red glimmer
dancing in the depth of the eye orbits.

Without hesitating Ema stepped forward, and snatched a brass,
art deco lamp from the nightstand and smashed it over the Horse

Creature's head. Parts of it exploded across the room, as the figure fell to its knees.

Ema turned and kicked the door between the rooms with a bang, pushing a second figure back into Ephelis' room. She turned to the first one who tried to regain its feet, even though a long crack fissured down the middle of the oversized skull. Despite the lack of emotion from a face composed only of yellowed bone, venomous intent shone out from its eyes.

Ep stepped forward and with the butt of his pistol viciously struck at the newly formed fracture. A puff of greenish smoke shot up from the widened opening and the body pitched forward, disintegrating before it hit the ground. The oversized head thumped onto the colorful rug with a note of finality.

Ep remembered the horse skulls he'd come upon in the desert sands as a child.

Ema opened the door to Ep's room. It was empty. The window stood wide open, the cool desert air smelling of dust and newly lit wood fires swirled inside, lifting the edge of the curtain drawn to one side of it.

"Where is the other one?" Ep asked cautiously, eyeing the dark corners of the room as he spoke.

"Gone. They sent them with hopes they could take you while you were alone."

"But they don't want to tangle with you?"

"No, but I believe their aim is to kidnap instead of kill you."

Ep walked over to the open window. Only his truck, parked where Ema had left it, occupied the passageway between the grounds of the hotel and a road empty of traffic. Beyond it, scrub decorated a landscape where the sun imitating a half-orange sunk into the earth.

He turned back to Ema and asked, "Kidnap me, for what?"

"It's not for money, or to claim your soul. There is only one thing they want, which is your body."

"My body?"

"To use it Ep, as an avatar, or a pocket."

"Like a puppet?" he asked in astonishment.

Ema nodded.

"You would never willingly grant them use of it, so they must dispatch your spirit elsewhere."

"But why me, I'm just an old policeman?"

"It's not what you are, but who. Ep what they want is your identity."

The man stood silent, pondering what Ema said moments before. "A disguise then?" He stopped, following the trail where this led. "I can only think of two people who don't know me well enough to be fooled by this."

Ema arched one eyebrow, encouraging him towards the answer he sought.

"Rachel and Joanne? But what do they need me for?"

"Now their protector is someone they fear even more than me. All they have to do is lure her away for a moment from his side."

"It's Rachel they want. She's my brother's child, a Lentigo by blood. Did I lead them to her?"

"Yes, unintentionally, but now that you found her, you are able to act as her protector. Eventually they would have come after her."

"How can I protect her now?"

"By hunting the hunter," Ema answered him.

"So when do we go hunting?" Ep asked with a look of determination in his blue eyes.

"Tonight we'll go, but for my disguise."

* * *

141

Absalom Sparks, former cowboy, rodeo performer and lastly western movie stuntman slouched in the murkiness cast by a building towering over his head.

Broad-shouldered and clean shaven, he could have passed for any handsome actor that found fame in the burgeoning western movie industry in Los Angeles. But there was only one problem, Absalom wasn't that intelligent, and his memory at best was slipshod, so learning lines was out of the question. However for a narcissist with a cruel streak, it was a bitter pill to swallow. When a movie set assistant pointed it out, he punched the man in the face, knocking out his two front teeth. He escaped prosecution by boarding the first train out of California.

This was how he found himself back in his hometown of El Paso, once more occupying the lowest rung in a money-making industry. He watched with hungry eyes, as they pulled boxes of illegal alcohol from the back of a truck parked behind a basement speakeasy nestled between nondescript businesses. A stairway led to tunnels used for their storage. It grated on him he was just muscle and a lookout, hired on the cheap because he couldn't land a job anywhere else.

If only the bootlegger who picked him realized how inattentive and envious Absalom was, he'd have chanced being short a man. But bad choices don't always end in disaster, but paired with an unlucky coincidence, it did in the worse way on this night.

Rival gang members finished dropping off their own shipment at a nearby bar when the rumble of a motor echoed from an alley one street over. One of them exited their vehicle and reconnoitered from the opposite end where Absalom pretended to be on guard. At this late hour there could be only one reason someone would park a truck in this place.

THE DEAD CAST NO SHADOW

Once the gang member returned, they made a quick decision to steal the shipment or at the very least destroy it.

Absalom Sparks, intent on imagining what new suits he could purchase if he had the money contraband like this would bring in, failed to see the shadowy figures that darted forward with stealthy steps.

Suddenly shots rang out, and several voices shouted out to take cover. Another spray of bullets echoed around Absalom. One of them ricocheted from the brick wall where he crouched, and he felt a deep, bee sting in his neck. He put his hand to it and the liquid warmth of his own blood poured between his fingers. He looked stupidly at the maroon wetness covering his palm. Another shortcoming Absalom had, despite his imposing physique, was that the sight of blood made him faint, especially when it was his own.

He fell backwards into Ema's waiting arms. The being once called Absalom Sparks watched in wonder as a beautiful, naked red-haired woman melted into his body. He saw his body stand up, remove a bandana he kept in his pocket and tie it securely around his neck, stopping the bleeding. He tried to reach out to what was once his body. His hand passed right through without meeting flesh and bone.

Stormy green eyes looked out from the familiar face he saw every day in the mirror. A voice sounded in his mind, "Absalom, look she's come for you."

The body that was him until moments before pointed towards a pinkish light that expanded and grew. There stood his grandmother, the only person he'd ever loved. She'd brought him up after his parents abandoned him. She died from a heart attack when he was fifteen years old, leaving him to fend for himself. Granny was the only one who understood it was difficult for him to learn what others did with ease.

143

Dressed in her usual flowered dress and apron she beckoned to him with a smile. He flew to her side, all the anger and heartbreak of his life melted away, as did the memory of his last moments.

In a few minutes, with no attempt to staunch the blood loss from the neck wound, his body would have died, but instead it became the pocket for the Walker Between the Worlds.

None of the men from either gang noticed the lone figure that walked away and faded into the blackness of the night.

A luxurious woman's slip left lying on the ground next to a puddle of drying blood mystified police who came later to investigate.

A Pocket by Any Other Name

Not too far away, Ephelis sat in his truck waiting for Ema to return. He gripped the steering wheel and tried to ignore what sat next to him until the animal stood on its haunches and sniffed the air outside. The black-tailed jackrabbit sat back down and stared at him, its nose still quivering.

They'd left the hotel and drove around until Ema indicated where they should stop. He wasn't sure where they were going, but apparently she did. She warned him to wait for her and upon opening the door of the truck, the biggest hare he'd ever seen jumped into the seat where she'd been sitting.

Before he said a word, Ema said, "She's here to look out for you until I return. I don't have time to explain any further right now."

A Model T with three men drove slowly down the street in front of them.

"I have to go now," Ema offered as explanation, before she stripped down to a thin slip. Her dress, coat, stockings and shoes she threw into the back seat. Without another word she walked off.

It felt to him as if time dripped like molasses on a wintry day. The unmistakable sound of gunshots echoed between the buildings down to where he waited. With Ema's words still ringing in his ears, he stayed put.

He saw a man's figure approaching. Ep reached into his holster and pulled out the pistol; his eyes never leaving the person who undoubtedly was heading towards him.

The man came to the opposite side of where he sat, stuck his head in through the open truck window and said in a gruff voice, "Ep, it's me Ema."

In shocked silence he allowed the muscular, young man to slide into the seat after allowing the rabbit to exit and disappear to God knows where.

He recovered and asked in a stern voice, "How do I know who you really are?"

In reply the man struck a match left by Ep's unlit cigar and held it up to his face. His chocolate brown eyes misted over and then became the grayish green eyes of his bodyguard.

"Enough said, where to Ema?" Ephelis replied, then stopped and continued, "Or whatever I call you when you look like this. Ema just doesn't seem right."

The young man smiled, "It doesn't matter, just call me Absalom."

The Unforgiven

Absalom tied a scarf around his neck in true cowboy style to cover the bandage peeking over the collar of his shirt. He was close enough in size to Ephelis that he could use the older man's clothing.

A few minutes later both men headed towards the Lentigo Mansion where they'd agreed to meet Celestino Garcia at 11 A.M.

A stocky man in a red, checkered flannel shirt held the gates open and waved them through. Trees lined an avenue leading to a Victorian mansion painted ochre with yellowish gray trim. Chimneys peeked out between the steeply gabled roof, and a rounded tower precariously held a widow's walk above it. Curving stairs led to a wrap-around porch and double doors.

Celestino waited for them with papers in hand.

Ep introduced Absalom as his assistant. When the attorney asked after Ema, he explained that she waited at the hotel.

They stepped into an echoing entrance hall that led to a grand foyer and beyond it a large, curved staircase. White sheets like immobile phantom draped over the furniture to safeguard them from dust. From somewhere in the interior a clock struck the hour.

Celestino explained that the recent disclosure of Rachel's existence altered the plans for the disposition of Edward's properties, but until they completed this Ephelis was the owner of everything.

Ephelis then gave him his son Patrick's address in Washington, D.C. and told him to send all legal paperwork to him since he was representing the Lentigo family including Rachel.

Celestino seemed surprised. "Your son is an attorney?" he commented questioningly.

"Yes, when Edward died, he was only a boy."

"Does he know about Rachel?"

"Yes, he knows everything, including our last conversation. He instructed me to ask you to send everything to him."

"I look forward to working with him." His tone was agreeable, but he didn't smile.

Absalom opened two large pocket doors that led into a sumptuous parlor. Over the fireplace a large portrait of a woman with glittering black eyes and a pale complexion dominated the room.

Her dark hair swirled in a regal pompadour style. A wide pearl choker fit around her thin neck, and her corseted body boasted a small waist and rounded bosom. The bright yellow gown she wore swirled around her feet.

To their unasked question, Celestino commented, "That is Stella Lentigo."

Despite the artist's talent, or because of it, the cruel lift of her slight smile and the haughtiness of her arched brow emphasized a personality used to getting her way in all circumstances.

The lawyer led them away, touring the house room by room. From a second-story balcony that overlooked the garden, they surveyed the manicured hedges. Absalom turned to Celestino and asked, "Is that a mausoleum under the shade of those trees?"

"Yes, it is a special request made by Stella. She wanted to be buried on the grounds. The only casket inside is hers."

"A little on the morbid side," Ep commented drily.

"In reality, more on the possessive side," Celestino said.

"Is that why the house has a reputation for being haunted?" Absalom asked in a subdued tone.

"Who told you that?" Celestino asked, but continued before getting an answer, "Never mind, it's just superstition. That's all there is to it. A large, empty house where every sound echoes; if the servants didn't make up stories, I would have been surprised."

It was at that precise moment that a loud thump sounded from the first floor.

All three men looked at one another in silence. Once again a strange rolling noise, followed by a grinding of stone against stone thundered from below.

"Is there a place we have not inspected yet?" Ephelis asked.

"Yes, the cellars. They stored the wine in one, and the other is for household items."

Absalom led the way down the stairs at a rapid pace, with Ephelis right behind him. Celestino followed, hanging behind, willing to let them encounter whatever created the disturbance.

Despite his dismissing tone earlier concerning the house being haunted, he'd kept to himself information about several disquieting episodes he'd experienced when inspecting the house by himself as part of his duties.

In those first years he would come when none of the staff were about to make sure the property was being adequately maintained. He often arrived late in the day after he left his office.

In the quiet solitude of the empty house he could swear stealthy footsteps sounded behind him. He could not shake the undeniable sense that someone watched intently as he went from room to room. The feeling was not pleasant but laced with menace and desire to do him harm. More than once he'd seen abnormally tall shadows flit around in the gardens.

Eventually he changed his schedule and only came the days the staff returned on their monthly cleaning jobs. He made sure never to be alone and more than once had to be the one to keep a level head when the servants ran out of the house after seeing or hearing something unexplainable. The same thing happened to gardeners and groundskeepers who described weird animal calls and what sounded like a woman screaming, especially around Stella's mausoleum.

They whispered amongst themselves, "La Llorona esta aqui!" The legend of the Weeping Woman was used to scare ill-behaved children, and that's what he thought it was… at the beginning.

More than once the groundskeepers would find the bones or decaying remains of animals throughout the property, more than could be accounted for by predators bringing their kill to the remote parts of the estate. He would give these men extra money to keep quiet, warning them he didn't want the women to become alarmed.

There was one man, harder and colder than the rest who would occasionally bring him bones that even he, with his untrained eye recognized as human. He admitted only to himself, the man blackmailed him subtly to keep the secret that not only animal carcasses littered the gullies that led beyond the property to the unforgiving desert that stretched away.

One day, another groundskeeper came to his office to tell him this man failed to return home. They had all been working at the house, and he stayed behind supposedly to retrieve his tools. He disappeared and never returned to his home. A few days later on a tour of the house to inspect the handiwork of the staff he found the man's cap wedged underneath the door leading to the cellar. He disposed of it and that was the last time he opened the door to store anything there.

He had no recourse over the years but to pay higher wages to keep the workers or attract new ones. The house's reputation never diminished, on the contrary the rumors increased.

Celestino in his mind justified keeping these events from these two men. He suspected the damage his credibility would suffer if he told them that for several years he made sure never to be caught after dark on the grounds of the Lentigo Mansion.

THE DEAD CAST NO SHADOW

They were waiting for him at the entrance of the cellars. He offered the key to the locked door. It turned with difficulty in the lock and Celestino said, "I have not been down here for quite some time. Since the upkeep has been in the other parts of the house, we've only opened the doors if there were any items to be stored there."

Suddenly the walls shuddered as if an earthquake rumbled beneath the house.

Absalom said, "Have you ever experienced this before?"

Celestino's voice trembled, despite his effort to keep it steady, "No, never!"

Once the door swung open, a blast of fetid smelling heat slammed against them as if it were a solid thing.

Celestino and Ep pulled out their handkerchiefs and placed them over their noses, it was only Absalom who walked forward to a landing where the stairs led downward. He clicked a switch and a dim light bulb turned on down below; it barely illuminated the entrance to the cellar which ran the length of the house.

Ep followed Absalom as he went down the stairs, and Celestino stayed behind watching both men descend. He didn't care what they thought of him, but he had no curiosity about what was causing this turmoil inside the house. The core of his being trembled with fear, urging him to get as far away from this accursed place as quickly as possible.

I Always Hunt

Absalom and Ephelis walked forward, threading their way through several boxes and pieces of furniture. Workers had left many of the items just off the stairs, as if afraid to go deeper into the recesses of the space.

Another set of stairs led down to another level of the cellar. The area opened up into a vaulted ceiling and in the middle a rounded wall protected a well. It seemed strange to find it here. Three steps circled around it. Absalom approached it and saw strange symbols etched on the lid which sealed the opening.

Lining the circular walls was burned out torches and below them manacles with lengths of empty chains. This was undisputed evidence this space had once been a dungeon.

Absalom traced the grooves on the well lid, and he realized it served the purpose of being an altar. The middle of it dipped inward where liquids siphoned towards the middle to fall into the depths of the well. Brownish stains lined the entire area, and he smudged the end of his finger with the powdered remnants. He murmured words that Ep did not make out, then he blew the dust into the air.

Suddenly a scream, of a thing, because it did not come from a human throat echoed in the subterranean chamber. Following it came a loud rattling that warned and expressed a great, endless rage.

The cover of the well heaved upward, settled back in its place but a rumbling could be heard coming from its depths.

Ep looked at Absalom with startled eyes. He only shook his head and indicated with his hands to wait.

THE DEAD CAST NO SHADOW

Another scream-growl erupted from the well, and the covering moved slightly. Long, scaly fingers curved around the edge and pushed it off. The altar piece pounded down to the ground.

The clacking of a thousand castanets filled the air, and a face both familiar but terrible emerged. It was Stella Lentigo, with yellowish-green scales that covered her face, neck and upper torso as she emerged from her lair. Her black hair once coiffed in the latest fashion of the day, spilled around her naked body in a tangle down to her waist.

Her eyes glinted with a golden light and the pupils were only a vertical slit. A forked tongue slipped in and out between her full lips almost seductively.

The odor that accompanied her entrance was the sickening sweet odor of rotting human flesh.

She blinked slowly like a beast awakening from a deep sleep. Her face was flaccid until she saw Ephelis, then she drew back her lips and the black interior of her mouth framed pointy teeth dominated by protruding fangs.

Stella hissed long, low and hard. She pulled herself out of the well with a second pair of arms. In place of her legs a thick serpent's body glistened with oily slickness.

Her attention centered only on Ephelis. He backed up but stood his ground; he knew that if he didn't face this nightmare, it would hunt down his family. But when it spoke, he summoned an untapped well of courage to stand his ground.

"You look so like him, you were his best beloved. If only I had the power to make him witness, the suffering I will inflict on you."

Only vestiges of humanness remained in her voice.

"What are you?" Ephelis asked, because it escaped his understanding how the beautiful woman in the portrait had transformed into this creature.

"I am what I have always been."

153

"You were once a woman and my brother's wife."

"This is the exchange I made to avenge your brother's betrayal, but they cheated me because of you."

"I only learned of your existence a few days ago."

"But they killed him thinking it was you," the creature snarled and ended in a low hiss, "both his body and soul were beyond my grasp then."

"Who wanted to kill me?"

"The castoff of the Lurco Demon, the one known as Levan Jackson." She lifted the tip of her tail and sounded the large, red-veined rattles at the end.

"Enough of your questions! Now you will answer mine. Where have you hidden the ill-begotten seed of your brother?"

"He will not tell you," a gravelly voice sounded behind the Stella Snake Creature. Out of the open pit emerged the emaciated form of Levan Jackson. He reeked of human feces and his body looked as it did when he died; old, withered and racked with pain.

Stella pointed at him and said, "He is now my slave, and I remind him every day in a myriad ways that because of his interference I lost my chance at revenge. His suffering assuages only a moment my eternal disappointment."

Ep shook his head, recognition shining in his eyes as he looked on the apparition of Levan Jackson who haunted his dreams only months before. He remembered the well-groomed and successful physician he met so many years before. To think this facade masked so much evil.

The Stella Creature slithered closer to Ep, "Tell me where she is. I have her scent inside of me, and I was so close before you spirited her away. Her and that whore of a mother. Give them to me, and I will spare you."

Ephelis stayed silent and once more shook his head. She came a little closer, and hissed, "If you don't, then I will claim you, your sons and their children. And I will return them all to that place where you escaped from when you were a child."

In response another figure emerged from the well. It was the hooded, yellow-eyed creature he'd encountered in the crypt hidden in the Concordia Cemetery when he was seven years old.

The Stella Creature grinned horrifically with a razor smile. It looked out of place on her scaly smooth face. "Yes, another of my servants, but an unwilling one. Unlike me, they do not hunt; I always hunt, that is why they all serve me."

If I Can't Have You

Ephelis' eyes were unwillingly drawn back to the thing he'd seen so many years ago that haunted his sleep during those years of his childhood. The creature spit and looked with hate-filled hard eyes at the Stella Creature, apparently it did not enjoy being under the power of another being.

In an unearthly tone it said, "You may be a hunter and all powerful, but you are not all knowing."

The figure placed itself between Ephelis and Stella, throwing back its cowl. A human's likeness emerged, its face full of rough scales and horned edges running along its jaw line. The yellow eyes gleamed with defiance. A thick lizard-like tail hung below the edges of the robe behind it.

"I have no claim on his family, and neither do you. Only I decide who I bring into my lair, not you!" His voice raged in a seething spit.

To Absalom, Ephelis said, "I think we better go."

"Do you think they'll let us go?"

"I'm not sure."

"I've seen their kind before, and I doubt we'll get to the door."

The Stella Creature stared with cold eyes; immobile as if she were a temple goddess made of stone, except her rattler clacked. She existed in a universe where suffering did not purify, but instead spread hatred, despair and anguish.

The sound of a falling stone coming from inside the well announced the exit of another being. This time it was the gargoyle, with burned nubs instead of wings who climbed out. He came to stand next to the Cemetery Guardian.

"Ephelis, I think we're officially outnumbered," Absalom commented.

"What I wouldn't give for a swig of panther piss," he responded. His mother always accused him of flippancy when scared, and this moment was proof he kept this trait beyond his teenage years.

Then he realized the voice that spoke did not belong to Absalom. He turned, and there stood Ema, encased in a blood-red armor that hugged her body like a second skin. The same as the day she battled the gargoyle, but now the colors that swirled on its surface deepened from maroon to bright scarlet.

She stepped forward, and whispered to Ephelis, "I must follow certain rules."

She planted herself in front of him, and said, "He will accompany none of you. He sought my protection, and I have granted it."

The Cemetery Guardian laughed in a mocking, slithery tone, "But of course Lady, I will not challenge you. He is yours." It retreated to the shallow steps surrounding the well. The gargoyle followed him.

Levan Jackson shuffled to the other side of the altar, also seeking to place distance from the woman who prophesied his hideous death on a lonely crossroad in Savannah many years ago.

The Stella Creature advanced towards her menacingly, but stopped when Ema did not retreat. She studied her from head to foot, sensing she treaded on unfamiliar ground.

"Who are you?" Her voice grated in the sudden silence.

"That does not matter," Ema responded softly, "I am protecting this man, and all of his bloodline. We are here to claim this property, and you will leave this place now. We can do this with no conflict; are you in agreement?"

Ema watched her features, expecting her offer to be rejected, however like a tigress suspecting a trap, the Stella Creature studied her closely.

A female facing another female; the possibility of an ally or an enemy still hanging in the balance. Truce or war, but in her core being Stella Lentigo always viewed other women as competitors she suspected would always win in what she desired the most, the ability to carry a child in her womb. Even though she was no longer human this fear and anger which corrupted her in life, spurred her every action to obliterate the essence of any quickening.

Ema met her stare unwaveringly, certain that the moment Stella died she made a pact with an evil force that transformed her into what slithered before her, because she wanted to exact revenge against another man who cast her away because she was barren. There was no moment she recognized her own self-hatred as the reason love fled at every instance from her life.

Learning about Stella's childhood from Delphine, Ema held no doubt she'd been molded towards darkness by events in her life, but like all beings she had a choice. Whatever pity Ema felt for her, she remembered the innumerable men and women who Fate had treated even more viciously, still ripped hatred out of their heart. Ema held no illusions this last opportunity she offered Stella to recant would end differently.

"Kill her," Stella instructed the Cemetery Guardian, "and make it painful."

"No."

Her tail drummed an angry tattoo. "You dare to disobey me? Will you tie your fate to these humans? It will be the worse for you."

In a sudden movement, the Cemetery Guardian, grabbed the gargoyle and dragged him to Ema's side. "Red Lady, I seek your favor. It was I who warned you. In exchange I ask you to release

158

me from servitude and I will give you this creature that was once human."

Ema stood and looked behind her. Ephelis with a blanched face stared at her unsure of what to do next. Near to him a yellow-eyed elemental guardian with a gargoyle in tow sought her protection.

There was only one thing left to do. "Levan Jackson, I will grant you safe passage to where you should have gone after the death of your body. Do you accept?" Ema asked.

The old man looked with fearful eyes at the Stella Creature. This was all the answer Ema needed. She motioned to him with her hand to come nearer. "Do you want my protection?" She asked Levan.

He nodded uncertainly, his eyes buried in wrinkly folds never leaving Stella.

"She will not let me."

"I do not believe she would be so foolish to interfere," Ema said in a soothing voice, then she turned to the Stella Creature, "would you?"

Internally she calculated who the creature would attack first. Would it be her, or one of the four who now sought her protection?

Ema understood the only thing that stayed Stella was that she was enjoying the cat-and-mouse game. Terrorizing humans and lesser beings inevitably became boring, and this obvious effort to goad her fascinated her.

A pinpoint of radiance hovered and within seconds expanded shedding a blinding white light around it. Out of the center stepped a petite blond, with a high-necked, Edwardian-style shirt with a beautiful cameo pinned at her throat.

She took Levan by the hand and brought him to stand next to Ema. He said only one word, "Annabelle."

The Stella Creature made to lunge at the shimmering woman, who winked out as quickly as she came.

Celestino Garcia followed Ephelis and Absalom into the bowels of the cellar, and had stopped at the top of the second set of stairs.

At one point he kneeled and crossed himself various times. Convinced his legs would not carry him very far, he didn't attempt to run away. The only person he recognized was Ephelis, and he saw the oddly dressed woman who came to his office the day before.

When he saw the array of creatures, he thought of all the times he wandered around the house by himself, and shuddered to think any of them were the ones that stared at him with such intense dislike.

The torches at the walls burst into flickering flames. In response a small colony of bats spooked out of their dark corners cried shrilly and took flight into another dark crevice of the subterranean space.

A terrible and predatory look came over the Stella Creature's face. The small coterie of beings she used to either torment or inflict the same on others were falling away.

Tired of debating with Ema, or perhaps sensing she was losing ground, she lunged at Ephelis. It was in that instance she understood why the Cemetery Guardian deferred to this woman.

She reacted so rapidly her movements were a blur, but the Stella Creature grunted as a grip around her throat choked her like an iron bar, not a human hand. The woman threw her backwards against the altar.

In a booming voice that sounded like breaking glass Ema said, "I granted you more than one opportunity to withdraw, but now you have attacked me and you will receive no quarter. We are enemies."

The Cemetery Guardian in his slithery voice, cackled venomously, "What an implacable adversary you have created. Seek no help from us in combating the Sibyl."

THE DEAD CAST NO SHADOW

The Stella Creature's serpentine features expressed a moment of surprise when she heard the Guardian refer to Ema as the Sibyl. She was puzzled by this. True to her nature she failed to admit she was not all-knowing.

Her four arms transformed themselves into hissing appendages that ended with snakes' heads, which complained loudly with forked tongues dancing in the air.

This time she attacked the gargoyle which towered over the others in the party. He bleated like a distressed goat, as those around him dove out of the way of the writhing snake heads.

A moment later, the serpent heads were twitching on the stone floor. Cauterized stumps still smoked where they once erupted from her arms. The stink of cooked flesh overpowered the already pungent aroma that drifted around them since the opening of the well.

Ema swung her sword around once in the air, and said, "The next time, it'll be your head rolling on the floor."

Stella's yellow-eyed stare followed the arc of the winking metal, and she sneered contemptuously, as long-nailed hands formed themselves from the burned stubs of where her arms ended.

Ema wondered if the Stella Creature realized the disadvantage she found herself in considering how many she had to protect. In her mind she ticked them off: Ephelis, Celestino, a disaffected Cemetery Guardian and his gargoyle minion, the lost soul of a murderer and necrophile and lastly the body of her non-sentient pocket hidden behind some boxes.

She didn't believe anything else would be seeking succor from the Walker Between the Worlds, but fresh on this thought came proof that she was wrong.

From the well, a wail of different voices echoed, however they all said the same thing in different languages, "Help us, help me.

161

Ayudame, socorro!" Interspersed were the moans of different animals.

The Purity of Fire

Ema's eyes met Ephelis'. She didn't need to be told these were the trapped souls of every being sacrificed and thrown down the well by Stella, as a human and later when she became a handmaiden of the devil.

The time of talking was over, and she rushed the Stella Creature who slithered by the well, guarding her collection of spirits.

She thrust her long tail in Ema's path, trying to trip her onward impetus. However Ema anticipated this move, since this creature was versed in attacking the defenseless but not defending herself from someone who wanted to lop her head off.

Ema leaped over the scaly thickness, and in midair swung her arm around and sliced Stella's head off. It rolled across the floor, the eyes still blinking and swiveling around. She kneeled next to the still thrashing body, and with the Iron Horse dagger she sliced downward from the neck, through the sternum and through the belly.

A green sludge erupted outward, and what followed was the naked, fully formed body of Stella Lentigo as she looked on the day she died. She hissed at Ema, but lay immobile as if unused to existing in her human form once again.

Ephelis came to stand next to Ema and looked down at the disemboweled body, and the woman who lay next to it with venomous intent shining out from her dark eyes.

Ema whispered words in a language he couldn't understand, only one word she repeated three times over, "Barachiel!"

A diffused light shone out from the opposite wall where blocks of stone seem to dissolve until a doorway appeared and a being stepped through it. The scent of flowers announced its entry into this world, and it inclined its head to Ema, who returned the sign of acquiescence.

She pointed to the well, and two other angelic beings followed through the doorway. One held a long-handled hammer which after a single swing destroyed the well. From it spilled the ethereal outlines of different people, including children and myriad animals, both domestic and wild. The other angel guided them in through the glimmering doorway.

In the incandescent interior, other hands waited to receive them. The stream of outlines finally faded out. The two angelic helpers walked back through the doorway

Ema approached the Cemetery Guardian and addressed the gargoyle, "I honor my agreements, and I protected you, but you have free choice. You can remain as you are or become what you once were."

It lowered its head, and whispered in a craggy voice, "I cannot remember who I was any longer."

"Let us find out who you were," she continued in a stronger voice, "I command you to remember!"

Its eyes closed, and the figure shrank, losing it gargoylish features, until what it left was only a man, dressed in dingy miner's clothing.

"What is your name?" Ema asked.

"Joseph Bach," the man answered and opened his eyes.

"Tell me Joseph, how you came to fall under the power of this being."

"I was greedy and foolish and abandoned my family in pursuit of finding gold. They were left penniless to fend for themselves. I squandered the money that by rights belonged to them so they would have food on their table, and a roof over their heads. Then I murdered a man who said he carried a map of where this famous treasure lay hidden. I got lost inside the tunnels and finally served the Cemetery Guardian in order not to die of thirst and hunger."

Ema raised her eyes to the angel Barachiel who waited patiently. "Will you accept him?" she asked. The angel nodded once and called the man Joseph Bach over, then passed him through the doorway.

"And this one?" She indicated Levan Jackson dressed in the rags they had buried him in. He hung back expecting to be rejected, but the angel summoned him, and with clumsy steps he walked into the brightly lit entry.

Ema turned to the Cemetery Guardian, who watched her with insolent eyes, because that was its nature.

"I will send you back to your place to guard the treasure that was cursed and given over to your care, only remember that you may not entice or trap any human. Only their avarice allows you to claim them. Do you understand?"

"Yes, just return me," it grumbled, because it did not like to be reminded of its limitations.

Ema took the Iron Horse dagger and slit the air, which opened into a darkness from which a swish of hot, fetid breeze flowed. With a quick push she disappeared the craggy-faced, lizard-like being. The tear mended itself in the Cemetery Guardian's wake.

From her place on the ground, Stella Lentigo watched with hatred and defiance. Ema came to stand over her, and spoke to Barachiel, "Send in the other angels."

The being of light faded, and the doorway dimmed. From the interior two tall and dark-robed angels emerged. Their ebony hair flowed in a warm draft of air that blew in from behind them.

Each one took Stella by an arm and helped her to stand. She laughed for a moment, then glanced into their faces and saw something that made her shudder. She tried to pull her arm from their iron grip, but they wouldn't release her and pulled her into the dark interior of the passage. The opening showed a dark door that thunked closed with finality and faded into nothingness.

Ephelis said, "Ema I don't understand why those angels from heaven are escorting her?"

She replied, "Who said they're from heaven?"

He stayed silent and turned to follow her behind several crates. On the floor Absalom appeared to be taking a nap.

Ema turned to Ephelis, "I don't have time to spare your gentleman's sensibilities, but we are beyond that, you and I, aren't we?"

He nodded, and in wonder watched as the smooth armor encasing Ema shrunk until it was only a blue cube vibrating in her palm. She stood before him in regal splendor of her nakedness. Then she lay on top of Absalom and sunk into his body with a violet shimmer.

Absalom blinked his eyes, stretched out and stood up.

With his man's voice he said to Ephelis, "You once asked me what I was, enough to say I am known as the Walker Between the Worlds and this is how I have existed for hundreds of years."

"Of course you are, and of course you have," Ep replied, thinking this was no more mind-bending than anything else he'd witnessed in the last few days.

They mounted the steps and found Celestino slumped on the ground. His eyes were closed, and he was mumbling a prayer. A sheen of sweat covered his face. He started when Absalom touched him on the shoulder, and he stood up. He stole a glance below, and sighed in relief when he saw the space was empty, except for the demolished walls of the well.

Ephelis asked him, "You said that right now this property belongs to me?"

Celestino look from one face to the other, and nodded slowly, "Yes, right now you are the legal owner."

"Absalom," he paused for a moment reminding himself that in reality he was addressing Ema, "burn it!"

"To the ground?" Absalom verified.

"Everything!"

Absalom and Ep looked at Celestino, who swallowed hard. "Whatever you want me to say concerning the fire I will say, just get rid of this place once and for all."

"Is there anyone else in the house?"

"No one."

Absalom escorted the other men to the other side of the cellar door and bade them wait. A few minutes later he opened the entryway once again and a blast of scorching heat came through. Before he closed the door, Ep and Celestino saw a furnace of fire engulfing the interior of the cellar.

They looked at one another, wondering how one person set a fire so quickly, but neither asked.

"Gentlemen, this fire will spread quickly so I suggest we get out of here right away," Absalom said in a calm voice.

Without further conversation, all of them quickly exited the Lentigo Mansion. Absalom and Ep in the truck, and Celestino in his own car motored outside the gates, and stopped to look at the thick column of dark smoke that rose in the air.

"The house is so far outside of the city, it'll take a while before the fire department comes out here," Celestino said in grim satisfaction.

"It'll be rubble by the time they arrive."

"I will take care of any explanations." Celestino whispered, looking at Ephelis.

The group of men watched flames erupt from the top floors of the structure. They drove into the city and Celestino accompanied the fire engine back to the site.

Night was falling when he stopped at the hotel and spoke to Ephelis and Absalom. He confirmed the Lentigo Mansion was only a smoldering ruin.

A Parting of Ways

The destruction of the Lentigo Mansion made the front page of the newspaper, but only because it was a slow news day, and its connection to Senator Gordon who died only two days prior.

Before the week was out, Celestino agreed to accompany Ephelis back to Washington D. C. to meet Rachel, and confer with Patrick Lentigo on the disposition of Edward's will.

Ephelis sold the truck to Absalom, and he drove both men out to the train station to start on the first leg of their journey.

Celestino oversaw the loading of their luggage, and Ephelis stood with Absalom. "Will I ever see you again?" He asked.

"Perhaps. If there is trouble, you know how get a message to me."

Ephelis lowered his voice, "Ema, because I know it is you who exists inside this man, remember that I too can offer you my help if ever need it."

"If I kissed you, it would outrage the public and ruin your reputation, so instead we will part with a hearty handshake."

"Where are you bound?"

"Albuquerque."

"Then Godspeed, Lady Sibyl."

* * *

Absalom fingered the brief message received at a lonely farm on the outskirts of El Paso. Unknown to all, except those who awaited messages via carrier pigeons, the missives received were for those who distrusted the telegraph and the telephone.

He read it once more. *"Sister Magdalen is on her deathbed and wants to see you."*

The last time she set eyes on Sister Magdalen was 1879. Mort rescued her from a demon attack at a high-end Barbary Coast brothel when she went by the name of Ruby Summerfield.

It was with her that Mort spent the last weeks of his life. There in a small garden enclosure she tended to his grave for the last ten years.

Ema acknowledged it was no coincidence that Mort came to Ephelis in dreamtime, and now she was being summoned to the place where he lay buried.

The handsome young man with sun-streaked brown hair known as Absalom brushed a solitary tear away from his cheek.

Ema knew what Mort wanted. He wanted her to make peace with his death, so he could find his own. But first she had to conquer this anger inside of her which she protected with every fiber of her being. It in turn did not let her feel the heartbreak of being an immortal human that fell in love with a mortal man.

The truck wound its way northward under the mid-afternoon sun, and a golden eagle flew above it, casting its shadow on the road before it.

www.ingramcontent.com/pod-product-compliance
Lightning Source LLC
Chambersburg PA
CBHW071914220626
47052CB00002B/339